JURASSIC DEAD 2
Z-VOLUTION

Rick Chesler and David Sakmyster

Severed Press
Hobart Tasmania

JURASSIC DEAD 2: Z-VOLUTION

Part 1: Mesozoic rising

1.

Washington, D.C. – 3 months after the volcanic eruption on Adranos Island. 9:45 AM.

Alex Ramirez left the United Nations special assembly council meeting after two hours of testimonies, questions and presentations to a select body of members, journalists and others. Frustrated and exhausted, he stepped out into the crisp fall air and a blast of bright sunshine, and for a moment he thought back to a day only a year ago, before the nightmare of Antarctica and Adranos Island, before… a similar release into a similar fall day. Only a year ago, after a week in a jail cell, locked up indignantly for a cause he championed but no longer remembered, only to be released with no attention, no fanfare or respect, with no one waiting for him on the other side. Not his father, who was off at the South Pole hunting frozen bones from distant eras, and not his mother, who Alex learned had paid his bail but was currently in her third round of chemo treatments, keeping her disease from the son she was likely too ashamed of at the moment in any case.

Now, a year later, the feeling passed, the *déjà vu* replaced by one glaring difference on this day of freedom: the steps were far from empty.

He walked into a dizzy greeting of the press, of cameras and microphones, snapping flashes brighter than the sun.

Alex held up his hands and then glanced around, expecting someone of far more interest behind him. He cleared his throat and decided to go for it. "What's up, people? Slow news day?"

"Mr. Ramirez!" Someone from Channel 7 thrust a microphone into his face. "Only three months ago, you sabotaged a Russian research facility in Antarctica and caused the deaths of over a dozen men, not to mention countless millions in lost research.

And now, instead of fighting for the protection of an almost extinct ancient life form, you're here arguing for its destruction?"

Alex sighed. "Sounds about right." He tried to sound as jovial as he could. He was tired, dejected, and had been through this countless times, his words falling on deaf ears. "As I've said to the Council, over and over, and to our government, to anyone who would listen…what we found in that lake is something I believe has the chance to unleash an unstoppable biological contagion on the world."

"Then where's the evidence?" a reporter from NBC yelled out. "Why isn't anyone acting?"

"Ask them," Alex insisted, even as something caught his eye on the street. A black limousine pulled up. A window lowered and a flash of auburn hair pulled from the shadows. "Ask them," he repeated, "about the restrictions and the zoning, ask about the private corporation the Security Council decided to grant full access, or how they've managed to deny any such site access to anyone else, including both the U.S. and Russian interests, tying up our efforts in red tape for months. Ask about…"

He saw the door of the limo open, and a hand emerged, waving to him. "Screw it, I gotta go."

He pushed through the crowd, broke into a run and then slid into the back seat. He slammed the door.

"'Bout time you rescued me," he said, out of breath. "This better be good."

Veronica Winters gave him a sly shake of her head. "Nice to see you too. Let's go, debrief on the way."

"Where to?" Alex held off the urge to sweep her into his arms. It had been too long since they'd been together, but the two sunglasses-wearing goons in dark suits sitting across from them were like bad-ass chaperones. Complete mood killers.

"Langley," Veronica said. "We've got some intel that might finally help us break through that red tape you've been on about."

She set her hand on his leg and leaned in, and right in front of the goons, placed a big kiss on his lips. "It really is good to see you. Now let's go, you won't believe what we've got."

Alex leaned back, smiling smugly at the expression-free faces of the other agents.

Then the smile vanished and for a moment he recollected the smell of sulfur and volcanic smoke, of blood and gore—and terror. Pure horror amidst the high-pitched screeches and roaring of things that should have died and stayed extinct.

"You know," he said quietly, "after what we've been through, I'd believe just about anything right now."

#

Langley, Virginia, CIA Headquarters. 11:34 AM.
"What are we looking at here?"

The speaker was a senior intelligence officer, Malcolm Nesmith, a hard-ass and pain to work for, but he'd gone to bat for Veronica on more occasions than she felt she deserved. She only hoped he could come through one more time.

Standing and taking up the laser pointer, she directed everyone in the briefing room to focus on the wall-length screen and the visual presented there.

"Satellite photographs from Oh-Eight-Hundred yesterday." She looked around the room at the familiar and unfamiliar faces. New blood and higher ranking intelligence agents. These were the people she needed to convince. These were the ones with the influence. What they said in their ops reports made it to the president's daily Security Briefing. So she had to nail this.

"We've been here before," a woman at the front of the table said. Debbie Harris, Veronica recognized her from previous briefing meetings. She had been a real back-stabbing bitch back then too, and no doubt was going to cause an issue now. "We know about your operation to Antarctica. About the unsuccessful investigation into William DeKirk, and your assurance that wanted bio-terrorist and murderer Xander Dyson was killed on some island in the South Pacific, but as for your other claims…"

Nesmith cleared his throat. "Let's not rehash the past, Agent Harris. This isn't about Agent Winters' vendetta against Dyson, as you keep harping on."

Harris glowered, her lips pulled back taught as her jaws tightened. Her slate-colored eyes gave away nothing as her voice bristled. "Xander Dyson killed Agent Winters' fiancée. It's only natural that we suspect our agent here of a certain lack of objectivity."

I'm right here in the room, Veronica thought, shaking her head. She looked to Nesmith for help, widening her eyes.

He held up a hand. "Just please hear us out. This has nothing to do with Dyson."

"But possibly everything to do with our initial objective," Veronica added, speaking up for herself. "DeKirk. You tasked me with tracking him down, something no one's been able to do in ten years. Why is that, by the way?" She asked the pointed question, glancing around at the faces in the room. Faces that looked down.

"Because," she offered, "he's better at hiding than we are at searching? Or because maybe he's isolated himself so well, and has the help of other countries, or possibly…other agencies?"

A man at the back looked up sharply. "What the hell does that mean?"

"Agent Winters," Nesmith snapped. "Stay on focus."

Veronica took a deep breath. He was right. As much as she wanted to vent her anger and lash out at this august group of know-it-alls—people who continually censured her and ignored her routine requests for follow-up missions and priority satellite searches— she had to stay on target.

And while her pleas had fallen on deaf ears for over three months, at last they had caught a break. Nesmith pulled some strings and got himself some time on the polar satellite. He surveyed the Lake Vostok area as she had been demanding. She would just have to focus on those findings and hope this group saw the same things she did. Maybe that would be vindication.

And maybe, she thought, *we're not too late.*

Before their rescue, she and Alex had agreed to get their stories straight. On the plane, flying away from Adranos Island, they had both understood that if they wanted the world to believe them at all, they had to stay on the right side of crazy. No mention of living, ravenous zombie dinosaurs. Focus on the biological threat. The microbes—or what did Xander Dyson call them?—*Prions?* Some sort of prehistoric protein, a failed or mutated enzyme string, complete with reptilian aspects which attacked a host body's proteins, turning them into structures like itself. Not just sickened, but *wrong*. Like Mad Cow Disease, this process affected the brain quickly, turning the intelligence centers, memory and speech areas to mush, effectively taking over and creating a mindless organism while firing up the hypothalamus to exaggerate hunger and accelerate metabolism, along with speed and strength.

That part they could talk about and have people buy into—they hoped. It wasn't stretching credibility too far, especially when instances of prion-related disease were out there already. Some tribe in New Guinea had almost been wiped out by such a thing in the 1950s. Of course that was because they had been eating the brains of dead ancestors, and all it took was one infected case. That was a little closer to the truth here, but again, by sticking to the facts about the biological threat—an ancient lake, preserved micro-organisms—the public could easily understand the potential threat if something we're unprepared for, something like that, was suddenly unleashed upon a world with no defense.

Alex had devoted the last three months to just such an effort, working the public, U.N., and state and federal agencies to warn them of the threat, doing everything he could to again—not sound crazy. Unfortunately there had been no evidence. Adranos Island was a burning pile of lava, fumes and wreckage. Toast from end to end after the volcanic eruption and the detonation of DeKirk's arsenal of munitions. No help there in terms of proving the more radical aspect of the threat.

Everything they would need to corroborate Veronica's insistence of a more far-reaching threat was to be found at the Antarctic site. Despite the American presence that had been there, racing against the Russians in a friendly competition to investigate the lake, the U.N. had promptly stepped in and isolated the zone in the aftermath of the accidents reported on scene. Both teams had gone missing, and reports of explosions and mass deaths had been confirmed. Then, to Veronica's dismay, the U.S. government had subsequently bowed to international pressure to back off.

"What you're seeing here," she said, regaining her composure, "is a satellite feed, two minutes in duration, over Lake Vostok in southwestern Antarctica. Only two minutes, during a window in which the usually thick cloud cover cleared up."

She wished Alex could be in here with her to see this, but he had been relegated to the waiting room in the lobby. *Eyes Only*, and despite all he'd seen, they still were not granting security clearance to a guy who had a history of eco-terrorism, a rap sheet and an allegation of international espionage against the Russians.

The people in the room leaned in, trying to get a better look. Agent Harris cleared her throat and said, "How did we get this? I thought by U.N. order 567-A45, no interference or surveillance of the area was permitted."

Yeah, Veronica thought. *But why the hell not, and what was that all about?*

Nesmith cleared his throat. "We had authorization. Leave it at that, Debbie."

Ha, he first-named her! Take that. Veronica's respect for her boss just doubled. Still, she recalled all the head-butting and late night arguments she'd had with him during the past few weeks before he relented. *Seriously,* she'd argued, *we've had the NSA spy on every foreign government leader and two-bit ambassador, wiretap and email snoop on everyone and everything, even U.S. citizens, but we can't check out a remote pile of thawing ice where there just might happen to be the greatest threat to civilization operating without the slightest interference?*

He gave her a slight smile. "Go on, Agent Winters."

"Thank you. Now as you know, by that same U.N. order you just referenced, access had been restricted since shortly after my return from the field. Not coincidentally, I would suggest, but as you've all pointed out, we've been here before. This time I want you to focus only on what we can see. And as you can see, there's a lot of activity going on down there at a supposedly quiet, supposedly restricted and potentially hazardous site."

She aimed the red laser dot at various points on the screen, allowing the agents to follow the movements of what appeared to be giant cranes here, ice drills there, bulldozers and pulley systems, hundreds of men, trailers and trucks, cargo containers and crates. Clearly an elaborate operation.

"And here," Veronica said, aiming the beam lower, "at the port. Notice what could only be called a *fleet.*"

"Jesus," somebody at the back whispered.

Several dozen oil-tankers, ice-chippers and two vessels the size of cruise ships. More in the shadows.

"What the hell is going on down there?" someone asked.

Agent Harris stood up, her bony frame blotting out the projector's light. She trembled.

"Agent Nesmith... We need to speak in private. Who else has seen this feed?"

"It's been seen by the right people."

She sat back down, hesitated, then got up again. "I need to make a call."

Veronica shot Nesmith a glance and he held up a hand. "People, listen. I've got this feed in the hands of our analysts and techs. They're going through the enhancements and trying to determine what's going on."

"What do we know about this GlobalSkyTech? The private company the U.N. contracted to take care of this site?" The question came from a junior analyst next to Veronica.

"Not much," Veronica responded. "I've been trying for weeks to get information on them, but all I've come up with is that it's a private shell company that's been involved in various international water drilling missions and salvage operations. Connections appear to be strong at the higher levels of the U.N."

She wanted to add more, wanted to pull up the flow chart that hung on her office wall, the threads tracing all the connections from this shell company to known DeKirk contractors, associates and business partners. Not to mention the one glaring and uncomfortable connection that it all led back to the current General Assembly Speaker of the U.N. However, Nesmith had made it clear: *stick to the facts*. Stick to what we could actually see. Satellite imagery didn't lie, and this...this unexplained and suspicious amount of activity down at the South Pole, where nothing lived or should be of this much consequence, was certainly unfurling some red flags.

Veronica shut off the projector after the video ran out. "Again," she said, silencing the muttering and shared whispers around the room, "this was taken yesterday. Since then, we have had no eyes on the situation. No idea if those tankers have been filled and, if so, with what. No idea if they've left, and for where, but we need to know. We need that authorization. We need birds in the sky, fish in the sea, we need that surveillance detail, and I would suggest…"

Nesmith cut her off before she could say it by raising his hand.

She couldn't resist though, and continued anyway. "The Arleigh-Burke class destroyer *USS Montana* is off the coast of Brazil. It's the nearest presence we have, and I only mention—"

"Thank you, Agent Winters." Nesmith motioned her to the door, then took her spot at the head of the table. "I'll call a meeting to review in short order and we'll discuss next steps. Again, thank you all for your time."

Veronica glanced around the room, eyes settling on agent Harris, who stared at her cell phone, clearly eager for that meeting to be called. Then, nodding, Veronica headed for the door.

My part's done. The rest, God help us, is in their hands.

2.

Lake Vostok research site

For Glenn Taggart, who held the inglorious title of Chief Research Consultant for GlobalSkyTech, the past three months had been the longest of his life, and yet when he looked back on that life, he couldn't recall anything approaching the significance of what he had accomplished here.

He stood on the railing in the cold and bitter winds, braving the sub-zero temps and the icy air for just a few more minutes, watching the operation he had overseen close up shop. He smiled as the last cargo crates were loaded and the ice trucks roared away down straight roads toward the port and the last of the container ships, waiting for its precious cargo.

From the vantage point where his predecessor, Marcus Ramirez, once oversaw the raising of the first perfectly preserved dinosaur in history, Taggart smiled and let the cold do its worst.

This is history, this is evolution.

DeKirk had hand-chosen Taggart for this mission, entrusting him with the most vital of operations, and Taggart had risen to the occasion. He imagined himself no less than a demi-god at this point, a modern Prometheus defying the gods and their plans for humanity, digging up that which most would say should never be unearthed. Preparing to give a gift every bit as powerful as fire to the unsuspecting—but deserving—masses.

He smiled one last time before he worried his lips would lose all feeling. He had to go back inside and give the final status report to DeKirk, but just wanted one last fond gaze. Down in the pit, the excavation leading a mile below the surface, to that gloriously mysterious lake, its waters nurtured by eons of pressure and geological processes. A natural womb for the microscopic prions that drifted mindlessly in its nutrient bath, waiting...waiting for birth into the new world. Waiting for new hosts...

...and keeping a few cherished old hosts for the journey.

Finally giving in to a shiver, Taggart watched the departing trucks and could just make out the glittering lights from the bay, where the largest of the ships undocked and made its way out, carrying something straight out of a nightmare. Something that rivaled anything even Ramirez had found.

Taggart had dug deeper. He had figured, where there was one anomalous find, why not more? He explored the surrounding areas. The cliffs, the caverns and the lake's deepest fathoms. Taggart had sent out drones and expeditions, and they found all they needed and then some.

This area had been far richer than anyone had expected. In complete defiance of a century of theories from scientists and expert paleontologists— professionals who should have had more faith—Antarctica had proven to hold its own treasure trove of specimens, as if during the last extinction the creatures had come heeding some call, some primordial instinct. Perhaps, as DeKirk had theorized, the microscopic prions that had infected the specimens had driven their instinctual tendencies, urging them south like migrating butterflies until they had converged on this spot, the most likely place to afford protection amidst the drastically changing climate system. The one place they could literally disappear and yet remain frozen, waiting for a future thaw...

Waiting for their reign to come again.

Time for that status call, Taggart thought, reluctantly. *Can't keep the boss waiting.*

Besides, he was eager to warm up, take a much needed drink, and start the next phase of his mission, where he hoped to be right there by DeKirk's side, leading the world through the next great extinction and evolution.

It had already begun, and there was no stopping it now.

#

DeKirk's image filled the entire screen, and as always, Taggart found himself noting the subtle changes from when he had first met the billionaire. Certainly, William DeKirk had always been an imposing figure. Despite his age (late sixties?), the man had that weathered look that inspired followers. A leader who had been battle-hardened. Silver hair that was more lustrous than frail, chiseled features and a jaw line that accentuated his feral countenance. Only now, the skin was tighter, sharpened and with a sheen of almost metallic tint. His eyes—formerly like jade Aztec stones plucked from a lost temple—had crossed the spectrum into a sun-like yellow, with slitted pupils, like a selfsame snake god from those very jungle-enshrouded temples.

"Sir, I'm pleased to say that at this time, all our birds have flown the coop. As of now, Operation Vostok-Z can be officially closed. I await your further instructions on departure, and…"

"You're going to have company very soon," DeKirk said. He wasn't smiling, which unnerved Taggart and brought down his mood.

He was warming up at least. The cognac he had just sipped was doing its part in conjunction with the heat in his office, the office where Dr. Ramirez had made his discoveries and where his son Alex had first brought the astounding news that the *T. rex* (or *Z. rex* as they had taken to calling it now), was more than just a preserved corpse. So much more.

"Sir?" Taggart checked his monitors, the radar and the long-range scanners set to surveil islands miles away, which had served as early warning points that fortunately—due to DeKirk's connections on the political scene—had been unnecessary. "I don't see anything yet."

"In a few minutes you will. There's also an American naval destroyer breaking formation with intent to head to your location."

"We'll be long gone by then," Taggart said. Although he wondered to himself, did that mean the cover was blown? Were the political roadblocks broken and was their mission more in jeopardy that he thought?

"True," DeKirk said in almost an offhand, musing fashion. His voice sounded deeper, throaty and rumbling in a way Taggart hadn't fully noticed before. He shuddered again even as the heat flooded through his veins. Shuddered thinking of what he knew DeKirk had done—the monumental personal risk he had taken. Some thought it arrogance that went far beyond hubris, while others felt it was foolhardy and suicidal, but Taggart knew better. DeKirk never took a risk, in business, pleasure or science, without first being assured that the outcome skewed in his favor. After all, one didn't become a billionaire by being averse to risk-taking.

By the look of things, he had more than succeeded. Normally, the prions infected the brain foremost, and all the resulting ancillary biological improvements such as speed, longevity, invulnerability and immense strength came at the cost of destruction of various mental functions including memory, decision-making, logic and self-preservation.

DeKirk, however, had found a way to use the prions to get the best of both worlds.

Hopefully, Taggart thought with a tingling sensation that had nothing to do with the cold, *he's going to share that with me as a reward for this exemplary service. I could use an edge like that. Who couldn't?*

Yet, there was that nagging thought: he couldn't help but feel a little like Renfield, expecting Dracula to keep his promise.

Nothing to fear, Taggart assured himself. The mission was a success and there was no one else who had proven himself as reliable and downright essential. He tried to smile. "So if the destroyer won't make it in time, what is this other threat?"

"Not so much a threat," DeKirk said, "as a...well, before we get to that, what else do you have to report?" DeKirk backed up and folded his arms over his chest.

As always, Taggart tried with some subtlety to look behind DeKirk at his surroundings in an attempt to glean visual clues that would serve as some hint of his whereabouts. It was the biggest secret, and the only one DeKirk truly kept under wraps. Taggart understood: no one could know where he was, and it had always been that way. He was too valuable and had made too many enemies. This communications feed was routed through so many Internet hubs and shielded locations that not even the best hackers could untangle the threads and trace him back to his actual position.

Taggart cleared his throat. "We went over schedule, as you know, by just a few days, but that was due to the problematic extraction of the subject found in cave six-three-one."

That brought a smile to DeKirk's lips, and Taggart felt a lump in his throat as he glimpsed those teeth: razor-sharp piercers, row upon row, and a serpentine tongue caressing a double set of incisors. *He did that to himself!*

"Ah yes, my *dreadnought*. I'm expecting grand things from that one. You confirmed the state of its preservation?"

"Yes, even better than we hoped."

Taggart sat and tapped some keys, calling up specs and diagram. Multiple dinosaur species flashed on the screens: pterodactyls with enormous wingspans, smaller crylopholosaurs, several tyrannosaurs, a shark-like creature and a larger marine animal with a face like a trilobite, a triceratops and then…something much larger than the *T.rex*, a little longer in the neck, but its head more gargantuan, its tail wider and legs meatier. Bio-statistics scrolled down the side of the screen: vitals and prion concentrations.

"It's in great condition," Taggart reiterated. "Aboard the last cargo ship along with a cache of pteros and…" he read the manifest, "…twenty seven of our human volunteers."

He smiled at that term, but it was a smile born of months working with the specimens. He recalled the hours upon hours spent in the windowless room they called simply, 'The Arena.' A vault-like chamber where the human volunteers were transformed—injected and then set free. Experiments ensued, carefully tracking their stats and their transformation process, studying them with implanted biosensors. Everything from hypothalamus activity and brain waves to endorphin production and stomach acid levels after feeding. Strength, speed, reaction to various stimuli and food sources, and most importantly—how fast they could overcome and transform another host.

The need for food—pure hunger—was the primary driver of their behavior, but at the same time, there was restraint. Consume, yes, but leave enough behind to provide another host for the prions. The ultimate, and fastest, method of reproduction.

Of course, the most interesting tests happened during the last month. The experiments that proved DeKirk's latest and most advanced theory: that a sufficient instinctual drive influenced the ultimate behavior of the infected. A biological imperative, akin mostly to migration patterns in birds. Not a hive mind, but there was definitely something there, an organizational matrix, that DeKirk realized could be manipulated. Taggart didn't profess to understand that part, it wasn't his specialty, but he knew the tests he ran at DeKirk's behest had to do with magnetism and electrical impulses, and much the same way as birds are influenced by the changing tides and the earth's magnetic field, so could these prions be manipulated.

Controlled.

It worked, in small groups at first, and then en masse.

The effort initially centered on humans, controlling their behavior at basic levels, alternating between blocking and stimulating hunger. Gradually, the aims of the work grew more sophisticated. Directing multiple subjects to converge on one location, or to work together to achieve an objective such as climbing over an obstacle.

It worked perfectly on the humans.

Then, after significant trial and error, but ultimately in triumph—with the dinosaur zombies as well.

Taggart recalled the taste of the vintage cognac he had opened after the first time they had essentially remote controlled a pterodactyl to fly a prescribed course as if they were playing with a radio-controlled model airplane. He was now about to finish that same bottle in final celebration.

"We have achieved the impossible, sir." Taggart raised a glass to DeKirk, hoping he would get acknowledgment back in kind. *And more,* he thought, admiring those teeth again, imagining the power he had been witnessing all this time transferred to him, coursing through his own veins.

DeKirk grinned. "We have indeed. And celebration will come soon enough, but for now, we still have work to do. Everything to date has only been Phase One. We are not at the finish line yet, and we must ensure our secret isn't revealed before its time."

Taggart put down his glass, regretfully untouched. "I understand." He needed to get back into this discussion, eager to join in the next phase and eventually find his place by DeKirk's side. "So what about Phase Two? Patient Zero?"

DeKirk almost let out a laugh of joy. "Ah, my favorite part! Nothing like mixing a little revenge in with our efforts. Patient Zero is at our offshore location, and she is doing perfectly well. Almost ready for transfer back to where she needs to be to unleash our surprise where it will hit them the hardest."

Taggart nodded. "And Phase Three? Can I assume I will be there...with you to direct operations and track our precious cargo?"

"Our cargo," DeKirk said, leaning in again, giving away nothing, "will get to its respective destinations in due time, after events play out on the political and military stages as I've foreseen."

His eyes flashed and lost focus, as if envisioning a far off battlefield, or a war map stacked with friendly and enemy markers, poised for global domination.

"Now, back to that visitor you're about to have."

Taggart perked up. He was about to ask if it was his personal escort—a fast transport to get him out of this frozen wasteland and back to the world he would soon inherit, but then his radar systems signaled an event.

"It's showing up now. Twelve miles out, coming fast. A jet?"

DeKirk nodded, then reached for something off screen and brought it into view. A piece of meat, it looked like: stringy and red, dripping, with skin—human skin—still on one side. DeKirk opened his jaws wide, licking his lips.

"It's a bomber, Mr. Taggart."

Still staring at the red blip zeroing in toward his location, Taggart blinked without comprehension.

"I thank you for your service," DeKirk said as he chewed into the flesh, tearing the strip in half like it was a moist and tender cut of prime rib. "I hope you understand the need for secrecy, and the fact that you've done such an exemplary job." Chewing, swallowing. "You've extracted all we needed. Tested and perfected my army per my instructions. To the letter."

"To the letter..." Taggart said, still staring at the dot. Understanding growing now, realization that the dream was about to end. His wake up call only two minutes away.

"There can be nothing left to discover, nothing to find, nothing to challenge us one day."

Taggart swallowed. "You're going to destroy it all. The entire Vostok site?"

DeKirk swallowed the last morsel, licked his fingers and grinned. "All of it. Thank you again, Mr. Taggart."

Expecting something more, something encouraging or promising, or perhaps a big laugh and the revelation that all this was just a joke, Taggart instead felt that he had certainly stepped into Renfield's shoes.

There would be no transformation, no evolution, no future. Not for him, anyway.

Only burial and death beneath fifteen megatons of explosives and an avalanche of ice.

3.

Washington, D.C.—5:45 PM

The situation room buzzed with energy and excitement, and more than a little trepidation.

"What are we looking at?"

The president looked distinguished as always in an immaculate blue suit, crimson tie and perfectly combed hair, as if this were a State of the Union address instead of an eyes-only special ops update. He paced like a hungry tiger at the head of the table in front of the Joint Chiefs and a host of advisors and analysts.

On the huge wall screen, bisected six ways, one screen dominated.

Agent Nesmith led off. "Center screen is the one to watch. Our satellite's positioned to capture a region fifty miles north of Vostok Bay, Antarctica. That convoy of tanker and cargo ships heading away from the ice is about to run into the best in class of American naval might: The *USS Montana*."

"Hails?" the president asked.

"Unresponsive to all radio contact. Not even an attempt at communication. Furthermore, we can't locate any data on these ghost ships, either. No cargo manifests or crew rosters. The vessel registration trail is just a nested-doll arrangement of never-ending shell companies and flag of convenience arrangements. Led nowhere, but at the same time they don't seem to have broken any maritime laws."

"What about this…this GlobalSkyTech corporation? The goddamned U.N. speaker, what's-his-face, blocked us for months with this bullshit, promised he had this reputable contractor down there to investigate. We were promised transparency and regular updates, and as far as I know—unless you people have been leaving me out of the loop—we've gotten squat."

"That's all true, sir. GlobalSkyTech…" Nesmith shook his head. "We have a ton of information on them, collected by our agent here." He nodded to Veronica, near the back of the room, who waited nervously, eying the screen, hoping she wouldn't be called to speak again, not in front of this audience. To keep herself from getting too nervous, she occupied her mind by trying to calculate how much money the taxpayers were shelling out for this fifteen-minute meeting based on the pay grades she knew were in the room.

Nesmith went on. "However, all of it just leads to more questions concerning their nature, connections and motives. All we know for sure is that they have not been playing by the rules set out by the UN."

The president rubbed his temples and stopped pacing. Palms on the table, he stared ahead at the screen. "No word from the Speaker? I want him on the line now, before we sink his pet company's fleet and send them all to Davey Jones' Locker."

"Yes sir, trying."

"Try harder. I don't want to be on the news tomorrow explaining why we just murdered hundreds of civilian contractors without good reason."

"There's a good reason," a voice spoke up from the back of the room.

Alex stepped forward and Veronica winced. She had fought hard to get him access, promising Nesmith that he had taken them this far and Alex deserved to see the fruit of their labors, that he deserved some measure of justice for what had been done to his father. Veronica knew that only too well. She sympathized more than she could let on, knowing the pain of losing someone you loved right before your eyes, helplessly. She had to allow Alex this moment, and Nesmith reluctantly agreed, after Alex had signed confidentiality agreements and passed an accelerated security clearance process.

All Veronica had asked in return from Alex was that he stay in the back, out of sight, *and quiet.*

"Excuse me?" the president said as he turned. "Who the hell is this?"

Nesmith hung his head. Cleared his throat.

"Alex Ramirez, sir." Alex stepped forward and lowered his head. "I...voted for you."

"Thank you. You and fifty-one percent of the other eligible voters out there." The president looked around at his staff, then back at Alex. "And—?"

"First term only," Alex clarified. "Not second. I liked the other guy a little more, but that was in my environmental phase, and…"

"Alex!" Veronica hissed.

"No, let's hear the boy out." The president turned to face Alex. "I remember your name now. You were part of the mess down there at Vostok, and then the resolution, as it were, on Adranos Island. Quite a bit of scorched earth there, right? Nothing was left for us to be able to piece together and use to support whatever it is you claim to have found."

"Yes sir, and—"

"And your father," the president nodded. "Good man, brilliant. I followed his work, and I'm sorry for your loss."

"Thank you, but as I was saying…"

The president raised a hand, silencing him. He turned his attention back to the screen, where the lead ship continued to move unabated to an intercept with the naval destroyer. "So we have no intel on those ships, what they're carrying?"

Nesmith shook his head. "None, unless you count speculation from the only living witness to lay eyes on what was down in that lake." He pointed to Alex.

"Okay," said the president. "Talk kid, and fast. I know you've briefed my people on the nature of some prehistoric microbe?"

"A *prion* to be exact."

"A what?"

"I don't really understand it too well, either," Alex said. "It's a protein, a nasty one that attaches to a host and disrupts the native cellular components, even at a genetic level, corrupts them and turns people…well, into zombies."

The president blinked at him. The room muttered to themselves. A few smirks.

Veronica came up behind Alex and whispered, "Should have just said Mad Cow."

"It's sort of like Mad Cow Disease," Alex stammered. "But way freakin' worse. It turns people ravenous, and mindless. I saw it. The Russians were first, and then anyone they attacked…bit, or even scratched…would turn as well. Fast."

The president blinked at him. "You're not kidding me?"

"No sir. My father.. .was infected."

"And?"

"He shot himself in the head rather than let it take him over. He was one of the lucky ones."

The president swallowed hard. Turned back to the screen. "And those things...those prions? They were in the lake?"

"In the lake, and in...some other things too."

The president looked back, about to ask for clarification, but Veronica cut him off, pointing at the tracking display.

"The tanker—something's happening!"

#

Most eyes were glued on the main screen, but the other displays revealed different angles: one from the deck of the *Montana*, showing a hazy twilight-sort of sky, with windswept clouds over the approaching armada, a ragtag assemblage of flatbed tankers, ice-chipping clippers and larger cruisers all bearing toward the destroyer.

"Engagement protocols active, sir," said the chair of the Joint Chiefs. "Given the unresponsiveness of the entire fleet, their unmitigated attack posture toward an American defense vessel that has properly identified itself and issued warnings, we are in compliance with international law to eliminate them."

The president lowered his head, nodding. "To say nothing of the fact that there is... I grudgingly have to admit...the serious likelihood of a biological weapon of mass destruction aboard those ships. Given that, we cannot in good conscience let them pass."

The Commander-In-Chief sighed, glanced back to Alex and Veronica, then straightened up and gazed at the central screen: the destroyer squaring off against the closing armada. "Give the *Montana* clearance to open fire. Sink the lead ship and let's see how the others react."

The chair of the Joint Chiefs picked up a red telephone and gave the order.

Alex held his breath. Veronica moved closer and let her hand drift toward his, sure now that with everyone's attention locked on the screens, no one would notice this one tender display. Their fingers touched, then interlaced briefly. Alex was about to look at her, to make eye contact and see if they could draw strength from each other.

This was it.

Sink the bastards, Alex thought. *Drown them all at the bottom of the ocean where no salvage mission will ever reach. Blow them to pieces and—*

"What the hell?"

The president flinched, as did half the room. The other half had their jaws open in disbelief.

"Situation report!" he shouted. "What is that, what are we seeing?"

Nesmith struggled to find his voice. "Sir, I..."

Alex's blood went cold. Veronica was gripping his hand so tightly it hurt. "It's..."

On the peripheral screens, with feeds from the *Montana,* a wicked silvery blur slid into view, something like an enormous tusk that reared out of the water then slammed down onto the deck amidst planes and men and turrets.

Three of the screens turned to static.

On the main monitor, the satellite transmission captured the impossible. The water erupted between the destroyer and the first tanker, and something rocketed upward with the force of a launching missile.

"Is that a whale?" someone asked, without any degree of certainty.

Alex squeezed Veronica's fingers hard, then let go.

"I said, *report!*" the president yelled. "What's happening? Why aren't we firing on them?"

The commander barked into the phone, but just then his head turned and stared at the screen—at the whirling figure thrashing on the deck, snapping and whipping its tail and massive jaws. In the blur from the satellite feed, it was almost impossible to see with any degree of precision, but Alex thought he saw enough: *the telltale massive sail on its back.*

"That's no whale. It's a Spinosaurus."

"What?"

"I saw that thing enough growing up with my dad, who kept correcting me when I insisted that a *T.rex* was the largest meat-eating dinosaur ever." He swallowed hard and pointed with his free hand. "No, it was that thing."

The room remained in mute, horrified shock, while the president stared at the images. The rest of the cameras went to snow after a chaotic sequence of rapid blurs, crashing water, shattered metal and a crewman's mangled body tossed into the air—almost ripped in half. On the main screen, something like a giant lizard stood on the sinking, smoking ship and seemed to be digging into its metallic guts with its snout, all the while shaking its prehistoric head.

Then everything—the *Montana's* remnants and its attacker alike—sunk beneath the waves.

"Holy shit." The president looked back to Alex. "Perhaps you two better give us more detail on what really happened down there. And no more bullshit about proteins and microscopic bugs."

Veronica swallowed hard but stepped forward, keeping her eyes on the screen, where the maritime convoy continued on, transporting a cargo more deadly than anyone had dreamed. "Sir...we thought...we thought wrong. We thought there were only a few of the creatures, but now..."

Alex completed the thought. "We're all screwed if any of those ships reach land."

4.

Centers for Disease Control and Prevention Headquarters, Atlanta—5:45 PM

Dr. Arcadia Grey fought off the urge to throw the package out, or to call the bomb squad or the hazmat team. Her slender hands trembled and she felt as if someone had just thrown her a ticking time bomb. Director of Pathogen Research for the CDC, she was the main line of defense for the agency charged with defending America against all manner of disease outbreaks, pandemics, epidemics, infections, plagues, scourges, contagions and weaponized biological threats. Right now, she wished she could be anywhere else, or anyone else. Someone who wouldn't have to face this responsibility.

The parcel was addressed to her and wrapped tightly in a bubble wrap folder, but it was the return address that had made her wish she had never come in today.

A single letter—the letter D.

Dyson.

It had to be. That was the way Xander Dyson had always signed his correspondence to her, whether they were love letters, business propositions, or late night emails waxing about the nature of single-celled life and whether it sprouted consciousness or housed elements of a soul, Xander was always one for brevity in signing his name.

Or was it arrogance?

Arcadia didn't know, but that was long ago. A relationship she had ended in what seemed like a prior lifetime, after she and Dyson had embarked on radically different paths. Both geniuses and leaders in their field, they were competitors who had become much more, and at one point Arcadia even had dreams of a family and a settled future.

But that was all shattered when Dyson took his genius and his theories and meshed them up into radical notions about genetic superiority and making the world a better place through targeted racial manipulation. Bio-engineered diseases that would only affect certain ethnic groups, things like that. He began associating with dangerous new friends and attracting the attention of people who could—and would— cause exactly the types of mass plagues and extinctions Arcadia was sworn to prevent.

She had risen to a senior rank at the CDC, her skill and promise noted by the current administration, and she had been rewarded with greater and greater responsibility.

Now this.

What to do with a package from a bio-terrorist who just happened to be her former lover—and who, by all accounts, died three months ago?

The only thing stopping her from calling the authorities and having the package checked for suspicious materials—or burning it in the incinerator right now—was the recollection of something Xander had told her one night as they lay in his big bed, cocooned in silk sheets. He had said that she alone was the only person he trusted. The only one he would ever share vital secrets with, and if anything ever threatened her, he would ensure she had a way out. A *failsafe*, he kept calling it, but she knew what he meant: an antidote, or an immunization.

She knew he had been working on such things for all the wrong people. What if he had succeeded, and what if he then made good on his promise and sent her something before he died? Something that finally made its way here after...that island and whatever happened there?

She hefted the package, warning bells chiming in her brain even as she ignored them all.

She tore open the wrapping.

#

The gift—a thumb drive ensnared in gobs of bubble wrap— was in her computer, and the lone file in the only folder sat patiently as she hovered the mouse pointer over it.

What the hell is zrex_kilr.exe?

Having come this far and throwing caution to the wind, she clicked open the file.

What are you giving me, Xander?

Even as the outpouring of data, 3D models and cellular micrographs whipped across the screen, and more and more files were accessed, Arcadia knew her life was about to change forever.

She saw bits of protein strings whipping past her eyes, then flashes of still photos and video files depicting impossible things—things that could have been visuals out of a Hollywood make-up effects lab.

Unblinking, she took it all in, bombarded, mesmerized and overwhelmed, but her confusion and disbelief began to clear away as the scientific data began to roll out, reinforcing her deepest fears while presenting a compelling yet sobering scenario that quite possibly signaled a pandemic unlike anything humankind had experienced—far beyond Influenza outbreaks, Smallpox epidemics and the Black Plague.

She stared more intently at the data, and at the file directories, looking for the one that might represent the culmination of all this work. The antidote.

The 'Z-rex Killer'.

As started to search, her screen flashed and a popup from the CDC alert center startled her.

Her adrenaline spiked and her skin broke out in goosebumps.

High Priority. Washington had just sent in the alert. The equivalent of DefCon-5 or Terror Threat Level Red.

Arcadia looked out her window at the sudden flood of activity—all her friends and coworkers had received the same alert and now scrambled to make calls and warn their constituents.

The CDC was now on high alert for an imminent biological terrorist event.

Meanwhile, she had quite possibly just been given a gift from a dead lover that held the key to a solution.

First, she needed to make a call. She had to let Washington know.

5.

Langley, Virginia

Alex paced the floor inside what felt more like an interrogation chamber than a waiting room. He imagined there were cameras behind the walls watching his every move, and half expected that when the doors opened, the water-boarding would begin. Or the men with the white coats would rush in to take him away after he continued ranting about dinosaurs and zombies and evil plans to annihilate civilization.

He was still somewhat in shock that a room full of some of the most powerful people on the planet actually seemed to believe what he and Veronica had described, but he supposed seeing was truly believing. Especially when seeing a prehistoric sea monster cut through a naval destroyer and a contingent of highly-trained soldiers in a matter of seconds.

Before Alex had been ushered out of the strategy room, he overheard Veronica and the advisors talking hurriedly about defense initiatives, about aircraft carrier repositioning, about sealing off borders and putting the nation on high alert.

Alex had tried to butt in and tell them to make sure they alerted nearby countries. The coastline of South America for one—Brazil, Peru—any number of highly-populated regions could be hit first, and Alex could only imagine how fast the zombie virus—or whatever they should technically be calling this scourge—would spread. He could envision them losing the entire southern continent and then trying to contain the damage by sealing off borders, but could that even work?

Even as he ran through the scenarios in his mind, feeling helpless like a toddler standing before a towering unstoppable tsunami, he thought for the first time in days about his mother.

He hadn't heard from Elsa Ramirez in more than a week. After his return from Adranos Island and after the loss of his father just as they had been repairing old wounds, he had sought out his mom. Maybe it was the guilt finally settling in, or maybe it was just finally his maturity—or maybe it could have had something to do with surviving a string of brutal attacks from zombies and dinosaurs—that had given him new perspective. He had to reconcile with his mother too, while there was still time.

Veronica encouraged him, even insisted. Regret would be a lifelong scar on his soul if his mother passed before he could patch things up with her, before he could thank her for so many things, before he could share all that had happened with his father. Maybe, just maybe, his presence could even give her strength, help her beat the cancer.

So he had gone. It hadn't been easy, seeing her like that after so many chemo treatments and multiple surgeries. Not after he had been gone so long, and after being such a distant, ungrateful son. Not after putting the concerns of exotic species and microscopic life forms over the lives of his family, but of course, his mother hadn't seen it that way.

Surprisingly, and in a rush of emotion Alex hadn't expected, she had been proud of him. Instead of his father's initial shame and disappointment, Alex's mother greeted him with open arms and brought him into her little two-room apartment where to his shock, he found himself surrounded by a veritable resume of his life: framed newspaper articles, his diploma, even media clippings about his eco-warrior convictions were on the walls in places of distinction, as if his mother had been proud of his every misstep and had celebrated his flaunting of authority.

"You acted and remained true to your values," she had said as they sat and shared a cup of tea. "I didn't like you taking chances with people's safety, including your own, but you always did what you thought was right. That's how I raised you, and you never, ever let me down."

So floored by this, Alex could say nothing, but just wept and held his mother—bald and frail—and he wept even more, feeling her ribs and her brittle bones and knowing that he was going to be too late.

Far too late to this reunion, far too late to save her. Too late for anything but spending time with her, whatever time she had left. That at least was another value he honored, for her, breaking away only on rare occasions like today when his mission took him to the U.N. itself. Up until a few days ago, he had worked as much as he could behind the scenes, on calls and Skype and limiting face-to-face meetings to times when his mother had care or was in the hospital for overnight treatments.

Things had gotten progressively worse over the past few weeks, but surprisingly their relationship was the best it had ever been, at least as far back as he could remember, since when he was just a kid opening presents from Santa with his mom and dad, and everything was right in the snowy world.

Even Veronica had met her and spent some time—the three of them together, and sometimes Alex thought that without that experience, without Veronica living through it and seeing Alex's growth and dedication and compassion, maybe they wouldn't be together right now. Of course, he and Veronica hadn't had a lot of time together either, but that would come soon enough, once more urgent matters were settled. Once the threat was passed.

Alex's mother had been a priority, at least until today, until what just happened, but then—his phone rang and the caller ID showed him her name, and Alex's heart leapt. She had gone for another treatment, something new her doctor had suggested. Alex didn't know the specifics, and was taken aback that she had only just sprung this information on him while he was on his way out the door to fly to Washington last night.

He hadn't known where she was going, how she was getting there, or what was involved— whether it was a new procedure or drug or whatever.

So, dying to hear the details, he eagerly answered the phone.

He listened, his relief at hearing her voice turning to concern and then, crushing sadness and heartbreak as she told him the news.

#

Veronica found Alex in the waiting room, talking on his phone. His eyes brimmed with tears as he ended the call with a choked goodbye.

She said nothing, just searched his red-rimmed eyes as a lump lodged in her throat.

"How...how did it go?" he asked, wiping away a tear.

She shook her head. "You probably heard it all before you left. All the main stuff. We're locking down the borders, putting the navy on alert, redirecting the satellites and trying to get other countries on board with shared surveillance and cooperation."

"There's a lot of ocean between here and there," Alex said. "A lot of ports."

"Yeah, but we have a head start."

"You saw all those ships, Veronica. Only one needs to get through to a major city. Or even a minor one. Out of the thousands of ships docking every day, maybe tens of thousands. How can they stop them all?"

Veronica had to ask, and wanted to change the subject. "Was that your mom?"

His eyes fell.

"She...left the country three days ago."

"What?"

"An experimental treatment in Grenada. She just called from there, where they tried some last ditch cryo-surgical procedure."

"It didn't work?"

Alex shook his head. "She...isn't coming back."

"Oh, Alex." She went to him, slipped her arms around his neck and hugged him, just held him tight, feeling his chest tighten and his breath escape. "I'm sorry."

"I have to go," he whispered.

"No..."

"I need to be with her. At the end. She's completely alone. She needs me."

Veronica pulled back, stared into his eyes. "If you go, you may not be able to get back in. For I don't know how long."

"I know. But maybe..."

"Maybe you're better off there. Safe," Veronica said, nodding as if the debate was over. "Go, and let all this settle. We'll stop DeKirk and whatever he's got planned, and in the meantime, you'll be isolated there, away from any contagion, away from..."

"Dinosaurs and zombies who will be coming to devour the woman I love?"

She swallowed. "I love you too, but you're not part of this fight anymore."

"The hell I'm not."

"Way above your pay grade, sport."

"Really? I'm more experienced than any soldier you've got at taking out crylopholosaurs with a helicopter rotor."

She pulled away, and then held his hands. "I'll grant you that, but if they get that far again that you need to use such creative methods of dispatch, it'll already be too late. We have to stop them before they make landfall."

"We?" He searched her eyes. "I knew they'd want you, but can't you step away, too? Come with me, be safe and we'll wait it out, or consult with your bosses long distance. What does it matter if you're there in person?"

"Alex. I need to be here. DeKirk was my mission. This…this is all mine, no one has the expertise or knowledge base that I do."

"High on yourself much?"

"I'm not kidding. It's too late in the game to debrief anyone else. I need to be here at the heart of it all if there's any chance of tracking DeKirk and ending this before it gets any worse."

Alex sighed, and Veronica could see the acceptance in his eyes. He knew she was right.

"Go," she repeated. "Be with your mother, kiss her and give her my love, and… God, I don't know what to say at this point."

"You've said and done so much already," Alex said. "She loves you too, like the daughter she wishes I had been." He gave an emotional laugh. "I…"

Veronica leaned and stood on her toes, giving him a big kiss. "Get to the airport. I'll send clearance and reserve a plane for you. I'm assuming you can mark and track your own flight plan."

He nodded.

"Good, because we may need all the other pilots we can get."

"That's why I think I should stay," Alex said. "Or at least, can I come back and help out after…?"

He let that trail off, and Veronica shrugged. "Maybe, and yes you're right, we may need you. Stay close to a phone and be safe."

"You too." He pulled her to him and hugged her close, feeling as if it might be the last time.

6.

Underground Bunker—Location Secret

As he was prone to do of late, William DeKirk sat alone in the dark. The shadows and the lack of background illumination served to highlight the focus and reality of what he surveyed on the dozen or so screens on the wall in front of him, and the two more on his desk. A bank of servers and land-based phones occupied an alcove to his right while a great steel door stood guard at his back, behind a long conference table. Literal flesh and bone guards barred the entrance on the other side, but inside this room, he was truly by himself.

He knew he wouldn't be alone for much longer, so he planned to enjoy his last day of secrecy, seclusion and virtual anonymity, savoring every minute before the final thrust of his plan began.

Checking the status of his secure communications arrays and internet pathways—a tangled and complex routing of multiple hubs and locations, all built out from this site and expanded across far-flung geographic zones without anyone being the wiser—he smiled to himself.

This had been decades in coming, and his plan had always had just one blind spot. Actually not so much as a blind spot as what he liked to call a confident future opportunity. One he had been sure would present itself when he needed it. Of course, it didn't hurt to have a small army of bio-engineers, researchers and doctors all working on various pieces of a puzzle only he could see in its entirety. All he needed was for one of them to come up with the silver bullet—the ultimate weapon he would unleash to bring the world to its knees and allow him to step in and take control. There had been many other potential superbugs—viruses he could have tried, ways to an end—but he was ever the perfectionist, and decided to wait until just the right tool came along.

He was that confident in himself and his destiny, never doubting that he would find a way, and that when he needed it, a solution would present itself. All he had to do was nudge it along and make sure he was ready to act when he saw it.

Antarctica was the silver bullet, and what a bullet!

He still couldn't believe how perfect it all turned out. Flexing his right arm, he felt the flesh tighten, the muscle ripple. Felt the blood in his veins, cool and yet seething with energized power, and he shuddered. Giddy with the energy coursing through his body, he fit his right wrist into a device like a blood pressure cuff on his desk. Except this one punctured his skin in three places and took readings, feeding the results of his internal scan directly into the system.

Three treatments was all it had taken. Treatments that he once thought could have gone either way and could have just as easily ended his dreams and taken his life, except for one little thing.

Destiny.

It wasn't his fate to lose. It wasn't even a risk.

Nothing could stop him now, just as nothing and no one had come close in all these years of efforts. He had to laugh, thinking about the CIA, Interpol and many others who had been after him for decades. They had stepped up their search in recent years, and despite all their money, technology and legions of agents, spooks, and mercenaries, they hadn't even gotten a whiff of his true location or goals.

He cackled again, thinking about how he had always been six moves ahead of them, how he had eventually positioned himself to hide right under their noses. Only fitting that the hunters were about to become the hunted.

His vision lovingly caressed the visuals on the monitors, lingering a few moments on each screen. He watched the internal views of the tanker ships, where three crylopholosaurs and a Z.rex slumbered amidst a floor seething with human zombies, like dragons atop their treasure hoard. Another screen revealed a pair of chained creatures, enormous wings folded tight to their sinewy bodies, snapping at each other with long pelican-like beaks between incensed red eyes. The next monitor presented a deck-top viewpoint of churning waves and an immense titanium chain over the side, dragging along a beast with a serrated sail that thrashed and surfaced and dipped and snapped at the chain with monstrous teeth.

DeKirk savored each visual and felt his blood surge and his muscles harden, and more—he felt the hunger growing.

His stomach rumbled and his insides clenched and his mouth filled with saliva. This was beyond hunger, he knew. A rabid, instinctual *need to feed.* However, as bad as it was, DeKirk had his technicians modify the prion's molecular structure, tinkering here and there with its protein strands and inherent makeup, not unlike splicing genes. Once the feeding impulse had been isolated, it could be tempered. But first they had to attack and re-sequence the element that would destroy the host's consciousness and personality.

No point in becoming a god if you wouldn't be left with enough sense to appreciate your new position.

That part hadn't been easy, but thanks to Xander Dyson's initial research, DeKirk had been able to have his other brainiacs complete the task. At first he was worried about Dyson's rambling about a failsafe, and that perhaps he had been shrewder than he gave the man credit for, that maybe he had managed to get word to someone outside the island. The paranoid little freak would definitely do something like that, but DeKirk felt he could rest easy. Three months and no word of it? He would have picked up something for sure in all this time, and besides, Dyson didn't really have an abundance of free time last he saw the man. From the moment DeKirk had cut him off and left him to die, the biochemist would have been on the run on an island full of rampaging zombies and voracious dinosaurs.

No, there was no doubt; his failsafe died with him—if he even had one in the first place and wasn't bluffing.

Now, three treatments later, and DeKirk—the sole beneficiary of the zombie protein modifications—was on his way to perfection. By all projections, he should be fully transformed within the next twelve hours. Unstoppable, immortal and in control of all that power. All the benefits of being a zombie with none of the drawbacks. A god to a new race that, he found, would answer to him through a combination of naturally-occurring electromagnetic field radiation that the prions used to communicate and control other hosts, as well as implanted microchip technology where necessary (as with the dinosaurs, which could be overly unruly and chaotic without properly directed discipline).

Grinning, DeKirk flexed and then interlaced his fingers as he stared at another screen depicting some kind of medical chamber, where a frail bald woman lay on a table, IVs in her arms. A bevy of technicians stood around monitoring her vitals.

DeKirk licked his lips, anticipating the delicious irony to come. He had scores to settle with more than a few people, but this selection of Patient Zero would be a more than fitting assault on someone who had come oh-so-close to derailing DeKirk's ambitions—something not easily done nor readily forgiven.

One final screen captured his attention: a view from atop a mast looking down on a flat ship's deck where the largest of the lizards he had ever imagined lay strapped down, still in frozen slumber.

My dreadnought, he mused. At forty tons and twenty-five meters long, it was a smaller individual than some of the fossils they had discovered in South America. It had been found in a cavern, frozen almost throughout, just a short distance from Vostok. It had certainly been part of that same lake, lured there from whatever it had called home while the rest of the Earth began its methane or asteroid-induced climate change. Whatever it was, DeKirk didn't really care. Let the eggheads argue about what caused mass extinctions, because he was pretty sure he had the answer.

The prions did their work, and hunger did the rest. If an animal was hungry enough, it would eat anything—do anything—to sate itself and kill those relentlessly nagging impulses. A person would literally eat his neighbor's child, DeKirk had always thought, if things got bad enough. And dinosaurs, well...a mere reptile possessed not the faintest shred of restraint or morality. They were no match for starvation.

Hunger was the ultimate constant. Every species feared it, every organism experienced it at one time or another. Hunger drove migrations, and hunger—more specifically, the fear of it—gave birth to civilization, agriculture, and everything that came with it. Stars burned energy just as every organism consumed prey. A living thing was merely a biological machine, and machines must be fueled or they stop running.

Only now, DeKirk could control the perceived sensation of hunger in a zombified organism—human or dinosaur. Direct it, shut it off once necessary, once his goals had been achieved.

But first, he thought, as he perused his monitors once more, his army would feed.

And feed well.

7.

Grenada

Alex made a less than perfect landing, but a landing nonetheless. His late friend Tony's words came back to him from Antarctica, haunting him...*Any landing you can walk away from...*

He climbed out of the cockpit on the deserted airstrip, a little curious as to the lack of a reception. No maintenance people, no security, just the disembodied voice from the tower clearing him to land.

Curious, but not alarming. Yet.

He shrugged off the nagging concern and turned to the sound of an engine approaching him. The day was hot, humid and somehow overly dry at the same time. It was like his mouth was full of sandpaper filings and he had the unshakeable notion that trouble was coming, with his mother at the center of it.

Why was she here? Did it have to be treatment outside the continental U.S.? Was that all it was? During the flight here he had questioned everything. The tone of her voice, the timing of all this. Something wasn't right.

But now here she was, coming toward him. He could see her in the back of the Jeep.

Guess we're not going to the facility, he thought.

He took off his aviator's sunglasses, hooked them behind his collar and made for the ground transport, expecting to help her out. Instead, even before it parked, his mother—head wrapped in a yellow scarf, wearing tan slacks and a white silk blouse, sprang from the open door and ran to him. Elsa threw her arms around his neck and hugged him fiercely.

"It worked!" she yelled over the winds and the Jeep's engine. "It worked!"

#

"What do you mean?" Alex asked. "How are you better, what...?"

A thousand questions ran through his mind, along with a small nagging alarm bell which was subsequently droned out in a wave of excitement and joy. His mother was not only alive and well, but she was going to make it. A miracle had somehow occurred here on this little island.

But that warning bell chimed one more time. The coincidence of it all... She had suffered so long with this disease, but now that it had nearly run its course this mystery treatment works?

He pulled away slightly, and with a trace of terror, searched her eyes, then her skin.

"What is it?" she asked, her voice bubbling with uncontrolled happiness.

"Nothing, just..." He studied her features. Couldn't tell what was under the bandana-scarf, but she just seemed...healthy. A modest sunburn at worst, but her eyes were strong and vibrant, without a touch of (dare he say it) yellow or reptilian. *Why would he think that? Why consider that any miracle in this day and age had to come with a curse?* Couldn't it just be a modern triumph of medicine here on this island, far away from FDA rules and lengthy testing periods before new treatments and drugs could be approved?

"Did it really work? You feel better? I mean, you look great and all, and I am doing all I can to not drop to my knees and praise God right freaking now, but..."

She squeezed his shoulders and nodded fast. "It worked, Alex, and it's real, but..." She looked over her shoulder at the driver and the man in a black suit and sunglasses sitting beside him. "I wonder if something *else* is behind the treatment, behind my selection in the first place."

"What do you mean?"

"I've heard things while they thought I was unconscious. I heard your name, and something about Vostok."

Alex paled. *It is too good to be true.* "What else?"

She shook her head, leaned close and hugged him again. "Just trust me, we can't go back in there." She cocked her head back toward the facility. "I know you had dealings with these people down there. Your father too. Bad people, and I know his death was no accident. So I'm scared. I don't trust them, don't trust any of this."

She pulled away, locked eyes with her son, then glanced toward the airplane.

"Is it still fueled? Can we just go—how fast could we take off?"

"Mom, I don't know if we can. We..." *Shit*, he thought, looking at the driver, who now stood up and started to get out of the Jeep. There was a gun holstered at his right hip.

"Better not just yet." He stepped in front of his mother and addressed the men. "Hey there. I'm Alex Ramirez. Thanks for the greeting party. What do we do next? Is there a release procedure, sign out form or something?"

The driver said nothing, but the other man, still in the Jeep, lowered his sunglasses. He stood, then spoke into a walkie-talkie, something lost in the wind and the rustling palm tree branches alongside the runway.

"Get ready," Alex's mother said to him, over his shoulder.

"For what? What's going on here?"

"Told you," she whispered, pointing back toward the airport, "nothing good."

The man in the Jeep lowered the walkie-talkie and finally spoke, leaning over the Jeep's railing. "Mrs. Ramirez, Alex, you're to come back to the treatment facility for further observation."

"No." His mother was defiant, shouting the word as firmly as she could.

"Listen," Alex said. "Who's in charge here? I'd like to meet with him and review a few things. Including what authority you have here. Otherwise, I would like to take my mother home." He took a breath, and added: "Now."

"I'm afraid that's not possible." The man nodded to the driver, who then reached to his side for his weapon.

—only the holster turned out to be empty. A look of shock crossed his face as he looked down at the vacant leather accessory, then back up sharply.

Alex's mother stepped forward, raising the .45 and pointing it with both hands.

"Looking for this?"

"Mom!" *Holy shit.* "When did you—?"

"Not now. Alex, start the plane."

The man in the black suit shook his head. "Think about what you're doing, Mrs. Ramirez."

"Think about what *you're* doing. I'm getting out of here before you can do anything else to me."

"Like finish your cure?"

She shrugged. "I feel great, and I'll take that any day rather than risk whatever else you have planned."

"Mom..."

"You need more treatments," the man said. "Monitoring. We have to be sure..."

"I'll take my chances. I'll trust in how I feel, that whatever you gave me, it did the job. As to the rest of it, the rest of you...no way. I'm not going to let you hurt my son, or use me for whatever the hell you're setting up."

She aimed the gun, steadying her hands as the driver approached. "I mean it."

"Drop the gun, ma'am."

"Uh, Mom, maybe you should listen to them."

She fired, blasting a round right at the driver's feet, knocking him back in alarm.

Elsa screamed. "Call off the dogs! Tell your friends to turn back."

The man in black raised his hands in surrender. "Fine, you win." He mumbled something into the walkie.

"Now what, Mrs. Ramirez, since you have the gun?"

"Mom, really..."

"Trust me," she said, almost barking the command. "I feel right about this, just as I feel so wrong about that place. You weren't there. For days I felt like a prisoner, told nothing, just injected over and over. Put under and...I have no idea what they did. No one told me anything from the moment I got here."

"Okay, Mom. Okay." Alex had to agree at this point. She had stolen a gun and taken a shot. There was no way he was going to give her up and go back with these guys at this point, no matter what. *And the connections with Vostok, holy shit...* He reached out and gently took the gun from her.

"Let me handle this. I've had some experience lately."

He pointed at the driver, then the other man. "You heard the lady! We're leaving. Get back in your Jeep and turn around. Don't try to stop us and nobody will get hurt."

The man in black gave him a vile look, then lowered his sunglasses. "Whatever you say, Mr. Ramirez."

The driver went back to the Jeep as Alex backed away, his mother tugging at his shirt. They continued backing up until the Jeep advanced, then turned in a large half-circle and drove off.

"Now that that's settled," his mom said, "let's get off this island."

#

"We can't go back to the U.S.," Alex told her as soon as they were airborne. She gave him a worried, confused look but he shook his head. "It's all a big cluster—"

She narrowed her eyes and he stopped mid-curse. "It's all under quarantine. Feds issued a high threat level."

"Even for you?"

"Especially for me." He banked to the left and ascended, checking gauges and especially fuel reserves.

"We have enough to make Miami, but I know they won't let us land. Hopefully there's another option."

"Like what? Alex, I'm scared, but my, I'm proud of how you can handle this plane!" She beamed, even as she white-knuckled the arm rests in the co-pilot seat. Her gaze swept out over the crystal blue sea and the shimmering noon-time sky.

"Mom, thanks, that means a lot, but... I really can't process this yet. You're better, after all you've been through! It's beyond comprehension, but I'm not complaining."

"Don't. I've never felt so good. Other than a rumbling in my stomach—and oh Lord, why wouldn't they give me a decent meal? Just once, they could have offered me a juicy steak or even just a cheeseburger. I was so hungry..."

She licked her lips and Alex slowly turned and gave her a long, careful look before hitting some turbulence and wrenching his attention back to the flight path and the control panels.

"Ummm..." He saw something glinting up ahead, in the water. Something large. "Mom, what—"

The radio crackled and a voice shot out. "*Cessna 1104*, this is the aircraft carrier *USS Alabama*. Identify yourself and your passengers."

"Here we go," Alex muttered to his mom. "Wish me luck."

"*USS Alabama*, this is *Cessna 1104*. Alex Ramirez, piloting, I am returning to the U.S. from Grenada with one passenger and I request landing permission at the nearest air base, or—"

"Negative, Mr. Ramirez. You are ordered to turn back, return to your point of departure and await further orders or clearance arrangements."

"Uh," Alex said, "no can do. I have an elderly passenger with a medical condition and I'm low on fuel. Can we at least get an escort and a landing permit?"

An idea came to him, even though he had no time to consider the logistics. "How about we land on the *Alabama's* flight deck?"

"Can you do that?" his mother asked, eyes wide, leaning forward in an attempt to see the distant carrier.

Alex shrugged, then released the transmit button. "No idea, never attempted that but it can't be too hard, right? If those super-fast fighter jets can do it..."

"Negative," the *Alabama* barked in return. "Once again, you are ordered to turn back. *Turn*—"

The transmission broke off.

"What are those?" his mother asked, pointing down, out of the window. Alex squinted, wondering at how his mother could see better than he could, then his vision finally adjusted and he saw it: two smallish specks like birds circling around the carrier and above it. Then he noticed something else: a cargo ship approaching the carrier fast, like it was preparing to ram it.

As he was about to try raising the *Alabama* again, he saw things that awakened PTSD-like symptoms inside him: explosions on the deck, balls of fire and smoke erupting outward and upward, and as he closed in, bird-like shapes that grew and grew more detailed as they approached.

"Not birds," his mother said, her voice cracking in horror.

"They're dropping something on the carrier's deck!" Alex said in shock, watching payloads fall, then erupt into living, scrambling things—humans, he realized, dropped onto the deck. But not humans, he realized, seeing their speed, the way they hit the deck and then got up racing in all directions, hungrily hunting the crew.

"Not birds," his mother repeated in a hollow voice as they completed the first fly-over, zipping through clouds of burning smoke. The Cessna banked hard, and Alex tried not to get distracted by the chaos on the deck as he prepared for another pass.

His mother craned her neck and narrowed her eyes.

"Pterodactyls."

8.

USS Alabama—moments earlier

Major Casey Remington, thirty-one years old and just two weeks away from being a proud father for the first time, found himself thinking about, of all things, names for his future daughter. Olivia was due to deliver any day now, and under normal conditions, Remington should have been on the first day of his two week leave right now; they would be sipping wine on their balcony at their Kansas City condo, continuing their playful bickering about what name to pick, making sure it was insult and mockery-proof for school and beyond, making sure it was cute enough to be fun yet respectable if she grew up to make something important of herself.

Instead, this High Alert had gone out, and all the carriers, coast guard vessels, destroyers and hell, the entire U.S. Navy—every ship that could be spared—had been mobilized. All hands were needed to guard the borders. No ships got in, and all pilots were on standby. He had hoped being on a carrier would be deterrent enough for anyone foolish enough to dare the blockade, that whatever the threat was, it would surely seek out a weaker entry point.

So when he got his orders and he suited up to launch— preparing to intercept an incoming cargo vessel that hadn't responded to radio contacts—Remington was sure it was just a simple mistake. Someone asleep at the wheel, a trader with a malfunctioning transmitter.

Just a simple launch, flyover and report back mission.

Except it wasn't.

Ten seconds after he went airborne in his F/A-18, soaring up and over the Atlantic, he picked up a bogey at the same time his orders came barking through.

"Airborne targets imminent!"

What? Remington ascended, shooting for higher altitudes while zeroing in on the red blip, tearing in from the direction of the cargo vessel. *Could it have been launched from there?* Impossible! The specs on the boat were that it was little bigger than a freighter, and unless it had a heli-pad... No, this incoming threat—if that's what it was—appeared now in his vision, growing as he streaked toward it.

"Not a plane," Remington yelled into the mic.

One other pilot had launched with him, coming up strong on his right.

"Alvarez," he said, looking across his shoulder. "Take it easy and hold your fire."

"Ain't nothing but a bird," Alvarez shouted back, then eased ahead of Remington's ride. "A big-ass bird, but hell, that's all. I'll just..."

Another red blip appeared on the screen, this one coming up closer, as if it had been *underneath* them the whole time. *Impossible,* Remington thought. Nothing that big could fly under the radar, so close to the water, but yet...

Another bird?

He tilted the F/A-18's nose, then angled right as Alvarez streaked ahead—and Remington caught just a glimpse of something brown, leathery and enormous. Wings and a huge pointed head with a single searing red eye that seemed to look at him and up at the other plane simultaneously.

"Alvarez!" Remington felt a cross current— a sudden thrust from the creature's wings? He compensated, executed a full spin and turned, craning his neck—only to see the huge creature complete its missile-like approach and snap its jaws in perfect timing. Sparks and flames kicked out from Alvarez's left wing, where a chunk of the aircraft had ripped off into the attacker's mouth.

Alvarez got off a few rounds of machine gun fire, but then his smoking plane was nose-diving.

Get out, get out! Remington urged, horror-struck as he flew on and upward, away from the range of that...whatever the hell it was.

"Eject," he said in a hollow tone. "Alvarez?"

The other bird-creature came into view, flapping hard, flying lower as if struggling with a heavy weight. As Remington flattened out, turned and gave chase, he thought he could make out things in its hind talons—moving forms, arms, legs...hideous faces? He was seeing shit now, probably. Other figures clung to its body, grasping at gouges in the creature's flesh, passengers along for the ride.

Far below, Alvarez must have ejected. Remington could see the parachute open, a bright red, white and blue beacon floating to safety…

…until the first beast swooped down in pursuit, its giant wings blocking out the sight for a heart-rending moment, and then it was up and ascending again… this time, with shredded 'chute pieces hanging from its beak, and no sign of Alvarez.

The creature—a pterodactyl, Remington thought, finally putting a name with the monstrosity (*Names are important, Casey. That's what his wife would say. Let's pick one for your daughter already*) ascended, fast. Faster than he could have imagined.

He caught a glimpse of those crimson eyes and long-dead pupils, locking on to their next prey.

#

The next moments were a literal blur of clouds and sea, wings and eyes. Teeth and machine gun fire and maneuvers, the likes of which Remington had never attempted. His stomach was in knots and his lungs felt depleted, head throbbing with the pressure, but somehow he had managed to avoid the creature's first swiping attack.

Ascending until the pterodactyl tired, the stunt was basic Escape Maneuvers 101, but never in any training simulation could he have imagined this scenario.

"Command, what the hell is this thing?" *Where's the Intel?* Certainly the Brass had more information than they were sharing, and given what he had just witnessed, he understood the reluctance at revealing too much. Probably determined it would be easier to declare a general quarantine and blindly order an attack on disobeying ships than it was to sound bat shit crazy and go all SyFy Channel on them, spouting on about prehistoric monsters invading U.S. soil.

Leveling off at 40,000 feet, Remington looked back down, seeing nothing but the blue-gray slate of sea far below. On his radar, the blip was a fast-moving dot heading toward home base, joining up with the other dot that was already engaging the carrier.

"Command?" *Why aren't they answering?* "Shoot that bird down! It's carrying a *payload* of..."

Jesus, what in God's name was *it carrying? Infected humans?* Remington swallowed hard as he straightened out the nose, armed his two AIM-9 Sidewinder heat-seeking missiles and accelerated. "Command?"

"*Alabama* to Remington!" The voice was shaky, uncertain. "New orders."

"What? Sir, I repeat, two birds inbound to your coordinates, one carrying a payload—"

"We are on it, defenses intact and activated."

Launch some other planes then, damnit! He thought. *Take them out before...*

"Be advised, another plane is inbound."

"What?" He glanced over his shoulder—down, all around. Eyeballed his radar, then saw the electronic representation emerge, coming from the southwest.

"A Cessna, two Americans from Grenada demanding we either let them pass or let them *land*. You have to turn them back, escort them to...*holy shit, get—*"

The communication cut out.

In defiance of orders, Remington accelerated, closing on the *Alabama*, angling down and pulling up, coming in at a level approach until he could see something that chilled him to the bone.

A battle raged on deck. Marines opened fire on a ragged group of humans—humans that seemed to be moving way too damned fast, and somehow (did they have body armor?) they weren't even slowed by the bullets. He got a glimpse of a dozen marines swarmed and...shredded, just literally shredded en masse before his eyes, before they could react. Then he was past, zeroing in on the pterodactyls.

The one that had been chasing him was way ahead, near the bow of the carrier. It swooped down in what had to be a second attack upon the control tower, returning to finish the job. It landed on a broken edge, perching there as it shoved its entire beak inside, locked hold of something and pulled back in an explosion of sparks and something else—gore... As half of a marine's body flopped up into the air then down into its gullet.

Remington swore, lined up the creature in his sights, then riddled its body with machine gun rounds. Massive 20mm Gatling gun bullets tore through the thing's hide, shattered its spine and destroyed its wings, sending it rolling and screeching off its perch onto the deck where it flopped about, damaging three other waiting F/A-18s.

Feeling the first faint tinge of satisfaction, he banked around the deck, turning sharply for another pass to take a run at the human invaders—when he realized he forgot about the other pterodactyl. It was still there—higher up, flapping its wings, keeping itself in place.

Remington adjusted his sights, about to fire a Sidewinder when he saw that the creature still had its weird payload gripped in its talons, that only the stowaways on its back had been released to fight—still ravaging the deck and locked in combat with more marines emerging from their stations.

Remington hesitated. *Were they captives being extracted? Civilians?* He couldn't fire until he knew what he'd be killing.

And then there was his last order—stop the Cessna.

Damn. He took his finger off the trigger but flew by close, getting a better look at the beast.

He saw two things at once.

First, he was no expert in prehistoric biology, but the pterodactyl seemed to be more like a CGI monstrosity—all torn up in places, ribs and organs not only exposed but...chewed on. Its throat was slashed open and fleshy parts dangled from the open esophagus. Its neck and abdomen were clearly gnawed upon, with sizable chunks devoured.

Second, and the thing that made him regret not firing the missile, was that the humans in its talons—the humans that were dropped the instant he passed by—were in actuality far from anything that resembled human.

Whether or not they were even alive was questionable. Yet they squirmed, kicked and snarled, seemingly of their own accord. Then there were those eyes—hideously yellow, primordially vacant. They had fallen hundreds of feet, smashing to the deck—and instead of staying dead and broken, got right up and raced toward the nearest marines, those valiantly staving off other attackers.

Pissed now, Remington punched up the throttle. He banked hard around and zeroed in on the pterodactyl, which had turned tail and was flapping energetically, back toward that cargo vessel, probably for another payload, Remington guessed. He had to stop that.

He locked on and launched the heat-seeker.

Eat that, he thought with satisfaction as the missile roared free, leaving a glorious smoke trail. Resisting the urge to watch the attack to completion, he turned his attention back to the carrier deck, trying to locate targets he could strafe with the 20mm without hitting marines...but then he saw something that made absolutely no sense.

Marines attacking marines.

Without guns, the attackers moved with the same speed and ferocity as the uninfected marines, overwhelming their former comrades, falling upon them and... *Dear God...* eating them?

Still, Remington couldn't fire. What was this? A plague that acted so quickly, turning humans into...

He couldn't say it, couldn't think, but he had to do something. Maybe there were others still below deck, in the tower, the engine rooms? Comm was down, but if they could seal off the lower doors...?

No, he saw on the end of his pass that the hangar doors were open and a few stragglers were taking cover, shooting from behind crates as their former mates turned and rushed toward the sound of gunfire.

He had to do something. Flying over the smoking wreckage of the tower and the shattered wings of planes on the runway, he was about to make another turn when his brain registered an alarm, something not quite right. Not right at all, in fact.

The pterodactyl he had shot through with machine gun fire should have been lying there dead among the wreckage. Instead, it was gone, it—

Reared up in his view, drenched in water, ascending from the waves where it had fallen into the ocean. Very much animated, very much hungry.

#

Remington swore and banked hard, executing a dizzying series of rolls to get out of the way, just barely escaping from the snapping jaws as the creature burst into his previous path. Regaining control and pitch just over the water, he banked and ascended, and through his window he caught a beautiful, if distracting sight: the other pterodactyl was swerving and looping madly, trying to shake the missile on its tail. A series of swirling vapor trails marked its erratic path, but the outcome was inexorable.

Whatever these things were, even if there were undead, they still gave off heat due to muscle activity, and the missile's one track brain was just as hungry as its prey. Frustrated, the pterodactyl turned and snapped at the pursuing pest. Its wings were outstretched in an angelic pose and for a fleeting instant, Remington admired the creature's tenacity and poise, but then the missile struck home, detonating in the dinosaur's jaws, lighting up the sky in a frenetic explosion of blood, guts, fire and bone.

Suppressing a grin, Remington spun around and sought out the other target—the first monster's mate, flapping up heedlessly toward him.

Have some more, he thought, arming the next missile. *Game of chicken?* It only took a second, but time seemed to slow down as he felt drawn into the thing's ancient implacable gaze and had a moment's wonder at what vistas it had once seen, and the long eons it had perhaps slept, waiting for this day, when it would be destroyed by a technological marvel invented epochs after its birth.

This day, this instant, Remington simultaneously launched the missile and banked upward, then accelerated.

He felt the explosion, the shockwave rocking the rear of the aircraft. He stabilized, checked the radar and saw the blip gone, even as he turned and caught a glimpse of smoking wings fluttering into the sea.

Grimly content, he flew back around, heading for the carrier, which now seemed eerily quiet.

"*Alabama*, this is *Cessna 1104*," came a new voice on his comm. "Anyone out there? We are coming in, low on fuel, and need to land soon."

Damn it, Remington thought. *Forgot about that nut job.* He grabbed the radio.

"*Cessna 1104*, do not approach. I repeat, *turn back*. I am ordered to escort you from U.S. airspace. This is the last place you'd want to be, anyway, take my word."

"Please," came the response. "I'm carrying an elderly passenger, and we don't have fuel enough to make anything but the Florida coast. Unless I can try to land on the Alabama."

"That's a big fucking negative," Remington shouted into the mic, executing another flyby. He saw no activity, just bloodstains and one grouping of those human types who appeared to be feasting on a body. *Where were all the others? Inside already?*

His heart sunk. Then it was already too late.

Thinking of all his comrades, his friends for the past tour or more, some of them, he could almost hear the screams of terror and pain from below.

The transceiver crackled again. "Did you just shoot down a pterodactyl?"

"Yeah, two of 'em, and...listen, you might want to turn back unless you want the next one of those birds to crash into you." He could see the Cessna now, flying low, heading over the cargo ship—that silent interloper—and approaching the carrier.

"Sorry, I can't, and by the looks of things, the *Alabama* isn't a viable return for you either."

"What do you know about it?"

"More than you would believe. If the zombies are already on board, then the ship is lost, the men already turned."

Zombies.

"Jesus. Zombies?"

"You believe me, don't you? You've seen it."

"Who is this?"

"My name's Alex Ramirez. Radio ahead to D.C., or whoever you can get on the line. I need to land, I can help, but I need to be on the deck. Ask for CIA Agent Veronica Winters. She can confirm all this."

Remington flew under the Cessna, then up and around again, leveling off and doing a pass over the cargo ship.

He checked his missiles. *Shit. None left, or I'd take out that freighter, orders or not.* He scanned the deck and saw nothing; it looked for all intents and purposes like a ship on autopilot, aiming for a path around the *Alabama.*

"Goddamn it. All right." He ascended and caught up to the Cessna, then slowed to keep pace, leveling and looking to his right, into the cockpit where he could see the young man, and confirmed the elderly woman sitting next to him.

"I'm your escort. Don't leave my side until we land. If you deviate one inch, I'll blow your ass out of the sky."

"Gotcha."

"I will be calling ahead, verifying your story with that Agent Winters, and ordering a quarantine team and a squad of soldiers to greet you. You don't exit the plane until ordered to do so, and when you do you come out with your hands up. Both of you. Again, if you deviate…"

"Yes yes, you'll blow us to smithereens. Got it."

"Great. Welcome to America, kid."

He leaned back, shut off the channel and tried to raise HQ. One last glance at the smoking wreckage of the *Alabama's* control tower, then back to the freighter, continuing now unabated.

He had some really bad news to deliver, and if this was just the first wave of the attack, they had a lot to do to get ready.

9.

Fifteen minutes after the two planes left the smoking ruin of the *USS Alabama*, the freighter, as if remote-controlled, arced around the immense defender and its now undead crew. On the carrier, a row of zombies stood along the deck's edge, ex-marines and others, rocking slowly as they sniffed the salty, humid wind, staring off toward the Florida coast.

The freighter continued for a few more miles, reaching within twenty miles of the shoreline where Miami glittered in the sun's sinking rays. The ship traversed the serene waves, until the first drone aircraft zipped overhead and dropped its payload.

A second later the warhead detonated right on target—slightly off the freighter's bow, at a sufficient distance calculated to tear apart its aft hull, shattering its engine compartment and leaving it dead it the water, where it would sink with its cargo hold exposed and visible…for the second drone which passed overhead moments later.

The Reaper drone gathered its visual data and relayed them back to Washington, then veered slightly southeast—and readied its own payload.

Two warheads, launched with inhuman precision and cold indifference.

The missiles separated and streaked toward their shared target—the center of the *USS Alabama*.

The silent figures stood impassively on the immense dock, uncomprehending, unaware of their fate. Just watching with dead eyes and ravenous hunger that would never be sated.

10.

Langley, Virginia

After two tense hours of reviewing evidence, scouring satellite feeds, disseminating mission information and reviewing her former debriefing with the joint chiefs, military planners and the president's chief of staff, Veronica finally took a seat, along with the rest of the room as they watched the drone mission unfold in real time.

The smoke was still clearing from the bombing of the freighter, but on the split screen she watched with a numbness spreading throughout her body as the missiles took out one of their own— the majestic *USS Alabama*, sinking one the greatest assets of their own navy.

She watched in what should have been abject horror as the carrier split and the fiery halves tilted and sunk, extinguishing the billowing flames.

"Two hundred sixty lives lost," someone said, and Veronica knew that at last they all realized the extent of the contagion, of what they were up against. Those figures on the deck...nothing remained of what they were or had ever been. Their families would be told the truth: that they had died valiantly defending the homeland, and their bodies could not be recovered.

Veronica shook her head. "I still don't understand the enemy's tactic," she said, breaking the silence as she shifted her attention to the other screen and the debris field around the sinking freighter.

The Chief of Staff cleared the obviously large lump in his throat. "They got us to take out one of our own largest defenders, and opened up a path right now that we'll need to seal in. I'd say that was pretty fucking brilliant, as far as tactics go."

"Yes, but those resources—two pterodactyls and how many zombie soldiers lost?"

"Obviously they hoped to retain the air power, hadn't counted on our skilled pilot's fast reactions, but as for the foot soldiers...they can make more of them, and fast. An unlimited supply, if what you claim is true."

"Can we get a closer look at that freighter's wreckage?" Veronica asked, trying to peer through the smoke and the blurry image sent back by the drone.

"Working on it," someone said.

Veronica took a breath and glanced at some of the other screens in the room, including the largest one, over her right shoulder, displaying a map of the southern/eastern US and full of color coded lines and dots and symbols, indicating flight paths, vessel coordinates and locations of naval and Coast Guard blockades.

One of the techs came running in from another room. "Sir, we have a call coming in from pilot Major Casey Remington. Priority One. He's escorted the Cessna into Miami's auxiliary landing strip and is asking for support. Asking to speak with Special Agent Winters."

Veronica stood up. She had been following the approach with apprehension. She had told command that despite her relationship with Alex and his mother, it was inadvisable to let them into the country, and especially so after she was patched in to Alex and heard the details—something about a rapid escape from Grenada, from a suspicious facility and miracle cure. It all seemed too obvious, and yet—his mother had no symptoms. Still, they could check her out, quarantine her and Alex there and wait.

The Chief glanced briefly at Veronica. "No time. Change of plans. The president heard the situation and wants them delivered to our CDC branch in Langley. There's a biohazard team standing by. So tell Major Remington to transfer this Ramirez and his mother to his plane, refuel, and get back here ASAP."

Veronica winced. "Sir, I don't think that's a good idea to bring them here. Miami could work just as well."

"Sorry, but we don't have the facilities, and we don't have you. We need your expertise in figuring this out, and in debriefing her. Grenada? We looked into it, and it's completely off the radar. Whatever they're working on there might be connected to all this, and right now Mrs. Ramirez could be the only one who can give us clues. You know her, and so you can do the debrief and get us some intel."

"After making sure she's not carrying the prions," Veronica muttered.

The Chief nodded and turned his attention back to the main screen. He mumbled something to his aide, who fiddled with the controls and enlarged the view of the freighter wreckage to cover the whole screen.

He stood up along with half the room, everyone jostling to get a better view.

"What the hell?"

Veronica craned her neck, moving to see around a couple of analysts. "Oh shit!"

The water was littered with broken crates and smoking flotsam, but the crates that had opened had spilled their precious cargo. Cargo that now floated on the waves, floated for them all to see, drifting in mockery.

Hundreds upon hundreds of stuffed animals.

Veronica's voice dropped. "Birds?"

"Fucking penguins," said the Chief of Staff, who sat heavily in his chair.

"A diversion," Veronica said. "Jesus. All that...was just a diversion?"

She looked back to the screens of the blockade tactical positions along the eastern seaboard—and now saw multiple contacts breaking off from the stalled positions of incoming vessels. They streamed through softer areas and made a break for the coast.

11.

Undisclosed Bunker Site

William DeKirk watched the screens through the slots between his fanned fingers. With heightened senses and his brain in hyper-activity mode, he took it all in, feeling like he was a computer, calculating thousands of permutations each second for every action he saw, like a chess-playing computer plotting a dozen moves in advance for each one of his opponent's possible moves.

He watched the same screens Veronica was looking at, but from an opposing tactical standpoint, rooting for the little red bogies, urging them on, but knowing deep down that there was very little doubt as to how this ended.

The enemy had to stop each and every one of those intrepid little invaders, and DeKirk only needed one of them to get past the blockade and unleash its infectious cargo.

He liked his chances... He liked a lot of things these days.

Sighing, he licked his lips. He would have to call down for more food soon. The hunger, while temporarily in check with a host of enzyme blockers and neurotransmitter dampeners, stirred regardless. His stomach rumbled and his mouth watered.

Focus. There would be more than enough time to give in—occasionally—to the primal need and allow himself to gorge, to feel the bloodlust and satiating pleasure of tearing into the freshest possible flesh—live flesh—devouring the living amidst their screams. He had tamed that primitive urge for now—focused it, made it bow in service to the larger picture, to the ultimate feast.

The world would soon be his.

This ancient life form—well, it would have its wish. Its evolutionary paradigm would be fulfilled, despite its chaotic chemistry, despite its self-destructive nature. DeKirk had tamed it and given it the means to achieve its destiny—and his.

He watched, taking in the little dots of red, those that engaged the blue ones, those that skipped by on the way to softer targets, those deemed low priority risks. Not the big cities, but smaller, softer locations. Nevertheless, they were real places where real people lived. Real America.

Perfect targets, ideal footholds on the climb to conquer the nation.

His fingers tapped at keys to call up an overlay to the screen's real-time events: a projection based on his modeling program layered in with each team's mission.

Red lines streaked ahead from their points of origin. A good portion of them fizzled and winked out, expected casualties, while others dashed through unabated, touched down—and spread a crimson tide that gushed out in all directions, streaming faster toward the nearest populated center, then expanding and expanding some more. From the south and northeast, from the Mid-Atlantic, it was unstoppable once it began, expanding across the country until America was bright red.

DeKirk's saliva poured out now, dripping onto the keyboard until he noticed and pushed it away, licking his lips and swallowing.

Maybe he would call for an aide right now. Everything was going so perfectly, he could afford a little snack.

Besides, he thought, it wouldn't do to be distracted by hunger when the moment came, when the grand revelation and master stroke of his plan would finally be revealed, when he would announce his presence and his position.

The world would fall to the undead and undying.

12.

National Harbor, just south of Washington, D.C.

The Jefferson family strolled along a boardwalk constructed on the bank of the Potomac River. Peter Jefferson and his wife, Pamela, had a tough time convincing their two teenagers, Sandi and Aimee, to forgo their usual Caribbean trip to visit the nation's capital. Even now, walking past a row of touristy shops along the water's edge, it was clear the girls weren't thrilled with the decision.

"I sure wish I were lying on a nice hot beach right about now," Sandi said.

Peter raised his hands in a come-on-now gesture. "We've gone to the Caribbean every year for the last five. It's time to mix it up a little! And you know, with our last name, we must be related to one of the founding fathers. It's time to pay homage, am I right?"

"No." This from Aimee, the younger of the two by a year, who somehow managed to hear what was going on, even with her ever-present ear buds.

Sandi took over. "If we're direct descendants of Thomas Jefferson, then how come they won't put us up in the White House instead of staying at the Holiday Inn?"

"Well, I wanted to keep our vacay low-key, without all the paparazzi and media attention we'd have if everyone knew our true family heritage."

Pamela Jefferson looked out across the water, laughing softly to herself while Sandi went on.

"Yeah right, Dad. And that might not be so bad, anyway. Nothing ever happens around this boring old place, unless some nut job tries to jump the White House fence. I mean, look at this place, it's so tedious, there's—"

The water in the middle of the river began to roil.

Mom pointed. "Hey, there's something!"

"What?" Dad asked. The whole family looked out over the river at the disturbance.

"I don't know, it looks like something's coming up."

Around them, other people were stopping along the river to stare at the commotion. The leading edge of a ripple created by whatever was rising from the river reached the concrete seawall, gently splashing against it before reflecting back out into the river again. More fingers pointed toward the watery upheaval.

Suddenly, a wall of water surged forward from a central point, much larger and more forceful than the initial ripple. This was a wave, several feet high, barreling toward the river bank.

"I see a fin!" Aimee had actually removed her ear buds. Mr. Jefferson's eyes narrowed as he looked to where his daughter pointed. Indeed, a sail-like fin sliced through the water's surface, coming straight at them on the concrete river bank. His wife looked around, as if to see if she could find an indication that this was some kind of tourist attraction or publicity stunt for...for what she didn't know, but something, right?

Instead, as the first water was pushed up and over the seawall to rush up against their feet, she looked back to the river and watched as what was now clearly a gigantic animal of some sort rose higher from the water. Instinctively, Peter Jefferson began herding his family to one side, not knowing what they were facing but sensing it was best to stay clear.

"Look out!" a nearby tourist shouted to a kayaker on the river. The man in the tiny boat had been taking pictures of the boardwalk area and turned around too late to stop his kayak from being overturned by the approaching beast. Shouts of terror erupted from the onlookers as a giant mouth opened on the aquatic sportsman.

Even from this distance, the Jeffersons could see the teeth in that mouth. But that was not the worst of it.

"Something's coming out of the mouth, Dad!" Sandi observed the behemoth even while backing away. It bothered Peter to take his eyes off the overall scene and instead focus on such details as what was in the mouth of the thing based on what one of his kids said, but he did in fact see movement in there and...*holy crap!*

He watched in rapt disbelief as a couple of objects fell from the creature's oral cavity and spilled out onto the kayak. But as he continued to watch, mouth agape, he could see that they were no mere objects that had been disgorged from the animal's mouth—

no! They were...*people*? He didn't know how it could be possible, wondered for a fleeting moment if the water supply in the hotel had been spiked with some experimental drug by the government using its guests as lab rats, but after rubbing his eyes and taking a deep breath, he was all but certain. Human figures were dropping from the mouth of the...*dinosaur—is that what that is? Impossible*...

The kayak capsized as two of the humans toppled onto it and began grappling with the paddler, who began shouting for help. Cell-phones were produced by passerbys who dialed 911—or took videos. The Jeffersons began backpedaling for higher ground, unable to rip their gazes from the ungodly manifestation playing out before them. The beast kept coming toward shore after plowing over the hapless paddler. As it neared the seawall, it picked up speed, rising higher in the water. They could see its broad back now, topped with a membranous sail supported by rigid spines. It looked large enough to propel a good-sized sailboat were it to be placed on a mast.

Although, as Mr. Jefferson dared himself to look more closely at it, there was evidence of what he supposed might be damage: irregular holes in the sail; some were just thinning spots while others were completely missing the skin or membrane or whatever the heck it was. Greenish, sort of moldy-looking splotches covered most of it, but he supposed that might be from living in the water? Then he realized with a start that it was drawing very near to his family now and they had better move.

"Kids, Pamela—run!"

#

A massive, webbed foot emerged from the water and landed firmly on the concrete walkway with an audible *slap*. As it emerged onto dry land, a few more of the bipedal forms slipped off of it and began to stagger pell-mell around the boardwalk. One more dropped from the gaping maw of the prehistoric-looking beast before it, too, stumbled off as if in search of something.

People all over screamed in panic as the monstrous thing with its disgorged army of rotting humanoids took over the boardwalk. One young man stopped moving in order to take a cell-phone selfie with the beast in the background, and he was promptly knocked yards away with a vicious tail-slap from the dinosaur, which executed that movement surprisingly fast.

Over by a cotton candy stand, two of the zombies had surrounded a young girl and snarled and gnashed the rotten stumps of what remained of their teeth. She was alone, her parents inside a T-shirt shop just behind the candy stand.

At that moment, the first squad of National Guard soldiers who had already been dispatched from nearby on standby burst out onto the waterfront walkway.

"Freeze or we shoot!" One of the soldiers yelled at the two humanoids near the girl, but this of course had no effect. The rest of the soldiers, meanwhile, were awestruck by the dinosaur. One of them yelled the word "Spinosaurus," sure that he'd read that in the briefing. Something about a dinosaur larger even than the *T. rex*, but none of them cared what the hell it was. It was a monster and it needed to be stopped, and that was all they needed to know.

At least they thought it was. In reality, this particular Spinosaurus was no ordinary therapod, even aside from the fact that it lived eons after its proper era had succumbed to the ravages of time. It had been…zombified…for lack of a better term. Ripped full of festering wounds and reeking to high heaven of the foulest imaginable rot, it lunged toward the nearest contingent of machine-gun toting soldiers. Its lopsided, wobbly gait propelled it forward faster than anyone would have guessed, and even as the first slugs of lead pounded into it, the dinosaur was upon the soldiers, lashing out, screeching, spitting, flinging its tail.

The war had begun.

#

Pier Six Pavilion, Baltimore, Maryland

At first, no one heard the sound of the cargo ship's horn blasting over the strains of the pop music act careening on stage in front of thousands of adoring fans. They were an interesting act, the concert promoter noted—a Japanese export who played an infectious pop-metal blend that people could both dance and rock out to.

But right now their music was not his concern. Situated on a finger of artificial land that jutted into the busy Inner Harbor, most of the people faced toward the stage. Not the promoter, Jaime Perez, however, who stood just backstage with a commanding view of the act, his line of security guards in front of them to keep away the occasional overzealous fan, as well as the entire audience. Beyond that didn't usually require his attention, but right now he saw something that troubled him.

Jaime brought a walkie-talkie to his lips and held down the push-to-talk button. "Attention Harbormaster, attention Harbormaster, this is Jaime Perez, promoter for the act in progress at Pier Six."

He waited for a reply while he watched the industrial ship steam ever closer to the end of the finger of land on which the concert venue sat. He'd put on dozens of shows here and had never once seen so large a ship get so close to the venue. What's more, it appeared to be actually gaining speed as it neared land. No one except for Jaime seemed to notice, though, as on stage, the scantily-clad female pop star was engaged in a simulated sex act with one of her male dancers, the crowd reacting wildly with raucous shouting.

Jaime tapped his headset earpiece more snugly into his ear. "I say again, Harbormaster, this is—"

"Copy that, Jaime, we are attempting communications with the ship, thank you, over."

"Copy that," Jaime said, but thought, *Attempting communications*? He didn't see how they could have much more time to attempt anything. He could see a substantial bow wave pushing ahead of the ship as it continued nearer to the end of the concert venue.

Then, just as he was about to alert staff to get all people away from the area nearest the water, Jaime watched as a pair of U.S. Coast Guard cutters, painted in the distinctive orange-and-white motif, sped in front of the tanker. Still, the seagoing behemoth did not slow down. Jaime picked up his radio again and this time yelled for his staff to evacuate the waterfront. He couldn't believe how quickly the tanker had gained on the shore. Did no one see what was happening?

Jaime grabbed an assistant and told her to take charge of the stage. He left the backstage area and ran toward the far end of the venue, past the cheap seats all the way to the water.

He heard the screeching, wrenching, and tearing of metal before he got there. The rumbling of concrete being knocked into smaller pieces. The first shouts of confusion and fright, which would shortly turn to terror.

Jaime skidded to a stop once he saw that the ship was riding up onto the land, having impacted the seawall at an unsafe speed. From this distance, he could hear the Coast Guard cutters blaring warning messages through PA systems, to no avail.

And then the unthinkable.

A cargo door opened in the bow of the ship and...*no, it can't be*...Jaime had to consider for a moment if his water bottle had been drugged by some kid who would think that kind of thing was funny, or possibly even by a temp worker who wanted to get even with him for assigning him a crappy shift or some other perceived slight. This was a rock concert, after all. But no, he told himself after shaking his head. This was as real as it gets.

A dinosaur stood at the entrance to the ship's cargo hold. A *Tyrannosaurus rex*, Jaime was pretty sure. Impossible, though. Regardless, it was a fantastically large lizard, just standing there, stock still but for its nearly car-sized head which moved in small but quick, hyper jerks. Jaime wondered for a split second if it could somehow be a high-tech stage prop that hadn't been cleared with him. He didn't see that dinosaurs had squat to do with that little tart's act up there, though.

Then the prehistoric reptile set into motion. In one terrifyingly athletic leap, it left the ship and landed on the manicured lawn at the edge of the harbor's music venue. It raised its head up and down in rapid succession a few times, sniffing air redolent with the sweat and hormones of thousands of warm mammals.

Those fans in the back rows were pointing and shouting, many of them actually smiling, under the dangerously false impression that this creature was some sort of showpiece. That would be their mentality, Jaime thought fleetingly. And he couldn't blame them. They were here to be entertained, after all, not slaughtered by some weird animal. What in the hell was going on here? Because as he watched it, it dawned on him. This thing was real. It wasn't some animatronics model or holographic illusion as he had first suspected. It was alive!

But there was no time to ruminate on it, for at that very moment, a horde of costumed freaks, that Jaime at first thought were grunge rock fans who somehow ended up at the wrong show, but the shredded flesh and potent stench told him that this was something else altogether—ambled from the cargo hold, some spilling into the water and sinking from sight, but most dropping onto the lawn where they proceeded to spread out toward the crowd.

The people at the back of the open air venue didn't know at first what to make of it. A few turned and saw the newcomers, then promptly turned back around to the show, ignoring them. But most were curious, some actually approaching the horde, while others started to run. Alarm bells sang out in Jaime's brain, the potential for a panic situation that could lead to a human stampede at the forefront of his mind. He'd been in such a situation once before, many years ago, but it was something that as a concert promoter he was always afraid of. It was his responsibility to keep these people safe.

He barked into his radio for his head of security to stop the show. The crowd's reaction grew louder around him, and even with the earpiece in he had trouble hearing the radio reply.

"I said cut power to the stage, *now!*"

The response was hard to make out but he caught most of it: "...say they can't cut power with the cage dancers suspended...down first...do? Over."

Suddenly, Jaime was besieged by fans who saw him speaking into a headset microphone and pegged him for some kind of official. A woman clad only in a bikini ran up to him and clutched his arm, pointing frantically at the marauding lizard.

"What the fuck is that thing? Is that for the circus?"

The radio crackled again in his ear."...say again, boss...need to know...do?"

Into the mic, Jaime returned, "Shut it all down now—just do what you have to do, *over!*" He had no idea it would be the last coherent order he would give an employee in his life, that it really was all over.

"Hey mister, what's with all those homeless people who just came out of the ship?" The worried woman was tugging at him again.

He eyed the shambling mass of slovenly humans but something about them didn't look right at *all*, even worse than the dinosaur. He leveled a stare at the eyes of one of them and saw nothing there whatsoever. Not even a feral, animal kind of intensity. Only a deadness. He'd seen plenty of homeless and drug addicted people—some in this very crowd here today—but this sorry assemblage of humanity that had descended upon his venue was one hell of a motley fucking crew, that was for certain. *Ridiculous*, Jaime thought. He was making a mental note to call the mayor later to see if this was some kind of new social program where some other city had been allowed to dump their homeless here or some crap like that when the commotion of the *T. rex* preempted it.

The Mesozoic reptile rampaged through the crowd, crushing people as it loped onward without care as to who or what was in its path. Near the front of the stage where the crowd was thickest, a mosh pit had formed with a young man crowd surfing, being handed from person to person on his back. The *T. rex* bent down its mighty head, a head with a set of jaws and accompanying musculature designed by millions of years of evolution to rip and tear through the thickest of hide and bone, and snatched the shirtless man in its jaws. It reared its head back, crushed the person in half with its five-inch long teeth and flung his legless torso to the front of the stage, where the most fervent spectators hadn't yet noticed the commotion. The band was still playing, the bright spotlights blinding them to the mayhem unfolding, but now security guards were flagging down the singer, running out on stage while waving their arms for her to stop.

The crowd caught the bloody half-man, passing him over their heads for a few seconds before realizing he was nothing but a mutilated corpse that looked as though it had come through an aborted meat-grinding process. The concert-goers parted in a rush, letting what remained of the dead man splash on the grass.

Looking around, Jaime felt increasingly lightheaded. His venue had crumbled to complete bedlam in the space of mere minutes. Absolute pandemonium reigned in blood. Fans fought fiercely with each other as they battled to flee the property. On the JumboTron behind the stage, a close-up of a gore-drenched *T.rex* mouth with a hand protruding from its teeth filled the screens. Further back in the middle of the lawn, a circle of undead fell on a passed out partier, opening the woman's abdomen and flinging entrails everywhere, crimson-splashed faces looking up from her opened innards, like contestants in a pie eating contest checking on their competitors' progress.

Jaime took a last desperate look out at the harbor and saw one of the Coast Guard cutters engulfed in flame and black smoke while the other fired machine guns at the tanker. Overrun, Jaime was fell upon and savaged by a tall zombie, its gray skin sloughing off in messy sheets as it scrabbled with him after having taken a mouth-stuffing bite. Then Jaime Perez faded, succumbing to loss of blood.

The last sight the promoter would take in was a squadron of no fewer than six winged reptiles launching themselves out of the ship's cargo hold and into the crisp, Maryland air. He heard one of them shriek as it turned, heading south toward D.C.

#

Charlotte, North Carolina

Already a large trucking freight hub for the Eastern Seaboard, it was a little known fact that the small city of Charlotte was also the nation's second largest financial center after New York City. Bank of America was headquartered here, as was NASCAR and a host of other well-known companies.

Igor Starinskovy backed his eighteen wheeler up to the distribution center's unloading bay. An employee emerged with a handheld computer and consulted it while asking him what he was carrying in the truck.

"Consumer electronics, machine parts and domestic goods." Starinskovy stifled a yawn. He'd been driving since the previous night from the port of New York where he'd picked up the truck.

The worker checked his electronic manifest and nodded. "Go ahead and open it up."

Starinskovy nodded and moved to the rear of the trailer, where he keyed open the padlock and raised the retaining bolt. Then he swung the double doors wide open.

"Most of this stuff is bound for—"

He never finished his sentence, for at that moment a veritable herd of cryolophosaurs rushed toward the open exit. Large therapods, similar to a *T. rex* but smaller in stature, the cryolophosaurs featured a prominent, red fleshy fan on top of their heads, sort of like a rooster. Unlike roosters, they were formidable predators, although no one knew enough about their behavior to determine whether they hunted alone or worked together in packs. The twenty of them seemed to cooperate well enough to move rapidly out of the truck, however, interrupting Starinskovy's thoughts as to how and when these horrendous aberrations of nature had been substituted for his normal, everyday cargo.

Illogically, despite the absolute horror and mind-numbing impossibility of what he was seeing, the only thought rising in his mind now was: this couldn't be his fault. But the only thing that really mattered now was the herd of free-ranging dinosaurs that had somehow materialized out of his truck.

One of the animals' tails whipped Starinskovy as it leapt from the trailer bed. The driver was thrown into the loading bay's concrete wall where he felt his elbow crack with the impact. He screamed in agony, the searing nerve impulses overriding his thinking to the point that he did not even hear the loading bay worker calling, "What the fuck? Jesus... what the *fuck?*"

Another crylopholosaur jumped from the truck toward him. It leaned over in one fluid motion and positioned its jaws around the stunned man's head. Then, with an effortless movement of its powerful neck muscles, it lifted up, severing the worker's head so swiftly that his headless body remained standing for a few seconds, hands still holding onto the inventory computer until he fell forward onto the pavement in what would have been a face plant had his face not been sliding down the creature's gullet at that very moment.

Starinskovy saw what happened and chose to remain very still against the wall where he'd been thrown, suddenly forgetting all about the pain of his shattered elbow. *Fuck your stupid elbow. At least you still have a head. You still have a head, damn it! Use it if you want to stay alive!*

He started to reach for the 9mm pistol he had proudly received a concealed carry permit for a few weeks ago. But he arrested his own motion before even touching the holster. What good would a pistol do against these untold tons of ravenous dinosaurs? He didn't so much as breathe while the parade of reanimated Jurassic beasts poured out of the trailer. He knew that should even one of these horrible, ragged-looking creatures notice him and decide to approach, he was done for.

He wet himself, the warm stain on his jeans dripping onto the concrete.

One of the trailing dinosaurs stopped and jerked its head up and down. It turned around, its leathery footpads making a rasping sound as they slid across the pavement. Starinskovy started to cry as the lizard began to run right at him, like a ridiculously oversized bull toward a broken matador. Behind it, two more of the reptiles began to approach Starinskovy.

He reached down the rest of the way and unlatched his holster, removing the 9mm. With a last glance at the loading bay employee's decapitated body lying nearby, oozing a small river of chunky fluid, Starinskovy stuck the barrel of his pistol into his own mouth.

Three crylos ran for him now, accelerating as they drew near. He wondered fleetingly if it would be more painless to be crushed by them, like being struck by one of his own tractor trailers, but then glanced at the headless victim again and decided he didn't want that no matter what. *They say you can still see for a few seconds after your head's chopped off while there's still blood in the brain. That dinosaur probably swallowed his head whole...what if the guy could still see and think as he rolled down that thing's throat?*

Starinskovy clenched his teeth so hard around the gun barrel that one of his incisors cracked in half and the barrel cut open the inside of his lip. Then he pulled the trigger and his cranial contents were power-ejected across the concrete wall behind him.

The first of the dinosaurs reached its prey and scooped the dead but still warm body into its mouth. The second beast came and tried to steal it but the first one clenched down. The newcomer separated one of the legs at the hip and absconded with its long, stringy treat. The third arrived too late for any real meat and contented itself with licking the brain matter and blood from the wall while the rest of the pack loped off toward the city's center.

#

Port of Savannah, GA

An oil tanker steaming into the harbor at Savannah was not an unusual sight. Dozens of the industrial behemoths plied their trade in the harbor and surrounding waters dotted with oil rigs each day. This tanker, however, had been extensively retrofitted to facilitate a specific and unusual purpose.

It carried zombies. Lots of them. Hundreds.

The onboard oil reservoir had been drained of oil and, although it still reeked of petroleum, safety or comfort were not concerns for the tanker's passengers. Inside the oil tanker's hold, a crowd of undead milled back and forth in darkness with nowhere to go.

In the ship's bridge, Captain Ned Whittaker looked not ahead at the crowded waters of the inner harbor, but instead gazed upward, scanning the sky. He frowned, seeing no signs of what he was looking for. His radio exploded with urgent questions from the Harbormaster, and he could no longer put them off.

"Captain of tanker ship, *Gulf Oil II*, please respond. The harbor pilot has not been able to establish communications."

Normally, the captain would have ceded control of the ship by now to the harbor pilot. This time, however, that was not going to happen. Whittaker again shot a worried glance to the sky. *Where was it?* He couldn't ignore the Harbormaster or put him off too much longer before the Coast Guard would be dispatched to board him by force.

He squeezed the transmit button on his radio, his sweaty finger slipping off of it once before gaining a solid grip, and spoke into the microphone. "Port of Savannah Harbormaster, this is *Gulf Oil*

II acknowledging. Had a technical problem with the starboard prop that we wanted to check out, it seems to be good now, over." He craned his neck up once again to the sky.

Then a different radio crackled—this one a walkie-talkie on his belt. One of his crew asking if it was time to open the oil bay doors. He swiped up the handheld unit and barked into it.

"Not yet, Malcolm. Standby for command."

"Roger that, standing by."

Then the ship's marine radio: "Harbormaster to *Gulf Oil II*. Copy that. Sending harbor pilot boat to your port side now for boarding, over."

The captain clenched his teeth and yet again looked to the air. What more could he do? This wasn't going according to plan. He would have to call DeKirk, although it definitely wasn't like him to screw up on plans. Just as he lifted his cell-phone, he heard the faint *whumping* in the distance, but growing louder by the second. A grin crossed his face. *Finally. This has to be it.* Still, the port was an extremely busy area for air as well as vessel traffic and he forced himself to wait just a little longer to get a visual confirmation before giving his crew the final orders.

Looking through the windshield of his pilot house, he watched the harbor pilot's small boat approach his tanker. He had maybe three minutes until that boat would be alongside, but if this aircraft was in fact the one, as it should be, then that should be enough time. The engine noise from above reached a crescendo, and this time, when the captain looked to the airspace he saw it: a blue A-star touring helicopter, exactly the kind DeKirk said would be coming for him.

Knowing the chopper pilot would have visual confirmation of the massive oil tanker, the captain looked grimly ahead and then placed his hand on the throttle control. His radio was blaring chatter from the harbor pilot coming alongside, but he no longer cared. Nodding to himself, he shoved the throttle to Full Ahead, then grabbed his personal backpack from the deck and ran from the pilot house.

He'd already rehearsed the run from the pilot house to the helipad with a stopwatch and knew he could make it in just under sixty seconds. As he ran down a metal stairwell, he shouted commands into his handheld radio. "Caesar, you're almost clear to roll. Open the doors and prepare to transport your cargo." He heard the roger reply and reached a catwalk at the bottom of the stairs, turned and sprinted down the narrow straightaway. Everything looked good.

He was dubious about Caesar's chances to drive an 18-wheeler out of here once they struck the dock, especially a truck loaded with forty tons of something straight out of a nightmare, hopefully still tranquilized, and able to remain so for the three hours it would take to transport it to Atlanta.

There was one more piece of the plan, one that was far more immediate—and brutal. So much so that he shuddered at the thought of the release of the other 'crew' he had transported from Antarctica. He brought the radio to his lips once again while he trounced along the side of the ship.

"Malcolm, Malcolm, Malcolm, come in!"

"Right here, captain."

"Unlock the cargo doors for our guests, and then you know what to do. Get the hell out of there and meet me on the helipad."

"Aye aye, sir!"

The captain ran up another stairway, taking the steps three at a time and looked left as he emerged on an open deck. What he was trying to see was not difficult to spot. It was hard to hide that sleek black 18-wheeler. Although they did try. A black mesh tarp was hung over it to keep prying eyes in the sky from looking down. Having the thing inside on the deck itself meant for the duration it had been closer than he wanted, really, but it was his duty to ensure the asset was delivered according to plan.

Dreadnoughtus schrani was a newly discovered reptile from the fossil record, but of course DeKirk wasn't working with fossils. This was the real deal. A living, breathing dinosaur larger than a *T. rex*, larger than a brontosaurus, even. Even though it was a vegetarian, the thing was ridiculously huge, Whittaker thought, and he had been unable to keep from taking a glimpse or two inside during the trip. Just a few times, when Caesar went in to administer another round of tranqs…administered through a giant needle and a hose system.

Caesar was all set—prepped for his adrenaline-fueled mission to come. Malcolm on the other hand had the unenviable job of releasing the plague of zombies upon the Savannah populace.

"Let's go, Malcolm!" the captain shouted as he ran to the end of the dreadnought deck toward the helipad, where the chopper now hovered just above the red-painted H in a circle on the elevated portion of deck. His crewman acknowledged with a raised hand as he ran from the great cargo doors after releasing the chain and lifting one side so it opened with an enormous clang.

Whittaker didn't stick around to see what came out of there. He was being compensated well, and DeKirk was not the type to spare expenses or cut corners when it came to his enterprises, but this was no game, and nothing was worse than facing what was down there. He didn't want to think about the population, and what was to come, but as it had been laid out to him, it was inevitable. He could either be on the right side of this changing world order, standing with the protected, the victors…or be one of *them*: the prey, the food, the dead…and the undead.

As the helicopter descended onto the landing pad, Whittaker thought of what would happen when this mission was over, as long as it was successful—and why shouldn't it be with all of the extensive planning they'd done? He hoped he could get away from the mayhem and violence and rest somewhere away from it all. He didn't need a private island or a mega-yacht or anything like that. Just a quiet little cottage on the rocky Scottish coast where he could live out his remaining years in rugged, rustic solitude, watching the sunset each night with a glass of fine whiskey. Dulling his senses, drowning out the screams and the nightmares that would surely haunt the rest of his days.

Whittaker reached a ladder that led up to the helipad and started to climb. The roar of the helicopter was deafening now, but also very comforting, for it signaled the end of his journey. It signaled success. He topped over the ladder and emerged onto the helipad. One of the two crew besides himself—his chief mechanic, whom he meant to take with him on the bird—was already on the landing pad, hunched over against the forceful rotor wash. He knew the pilot wouldn't open the door without consulting the captain, so he gave the visual signal and the door was opened. The mechanic, a trusted DeKirk Enterprises employee for many years, jumped inside while the captain rounded the craft to get to the door. As he did so, he glanced off to his left, down to the deck to check on Malcolm.

This time, the sight was not nearly as encouraging. The captain shook his head in bewilderment. The 18-wheeler was revving its engine, but somehow Malcolm had gotten his foot tripped up in one of the chain links bolted to the deck. The captain watched him pry off one of his rubber deck boots in an attempt to pull his foot free of the chain.

It looked like it may have been about to work, but at that moment the shadows in the brig exploded in a rush of arms, legs, rotting flesh and razor-sharp teeth. In the days that followed, the captain would swear that he could hear Malcolm squealing out for help, even through the helicopter noise, but in seconds he lost sight of the crewman under the onslaught of dozens of zombie figures bursting out of the hold, and falling upon him, thrilled at the gift of a meal so close.

Whittaker turned away, looking past the ship, as the Port of Savannah loomed larger. The converted oil tanker was deep inside the sheltered waterway now, and a little Harbor Patrol boat squealed alongside the mammoth ship, light bar flashing, siren wailing. There was absolutely nothing anyone on it could do. Even emptied of oil, a sixty-thousand ton vehicle with existing momentum simply could not be stopped on short notice.

The captain turned back to the helicopter. Except for poor Malcolm down there, they were ready to go. Sure, there were a few lowly deckhands still down below in the bilge area, having been instructed to stay down there until landing in port, but they didn't speak English, were undocumented, and most important of all, not easily traced back to DeKirk enterprises. In short, they were expendable...and would only serve to whet the zombie's appetites after they had finished off Malcolm—or let enough of him remain to be reanimated and join the growing army before it leapt onto the Savannah port.

Whittaker climbed the helicopter's ladder, even as the stench of the living dead mob reached him. It was choking, almost unbearable—and it rose so fast after being trapped in that hold for so long. After a transoceanic voyage confined in an oil tank with no water or drainage, even on the open deck, the smell of rotting flesh mixed with caked-on urine, feces (the captain flashed on a vodka-infused card game in Antarctica during which he'd won a bet with one of the Russian soldiers that zombies do need to "take a piss," after he'd chained one up in the corner of the room and waited until it soiled itself), and blood was so revolting as to be an almost palpable, physical threat.

Whittaker stopped climbing about halfway up, reeling from the olfactory assault. He gagged, but pushed himself to resume his ascent. The pilot would have no qualms about leaving him behind, fearing what DeKirk would do to him even more should he fail to complete his objective. He turned back and looked down, one last time, to say goodbye to his ship, to the tanker and the dreadnought, and his eyes then locked on the dispersing crowd near the open cargo doors.

"I'm sorry, Malcolm," he said to the gore-stained deck and the grotesque bloodstain—all that remained of the man he had just so recently played cards with and shared numerous bottles of vodka.

The captain climbed two more rungs and motioned up to the pilot to lift away. The rotor whine increased in pitch and the helicopter began rising from the deck. Suddenly, Malcolm was there—at the bottom of the ladder, leading the pack of the undead, having pulled away from them. Whittaker marveled at the ability of the corpse to even move, as badly devoured and shredded as it was: right leg stripped almost entirely of flesh below the knee, abdomen torn open and insides all but devoured, revealing the bony pelvis and spinal column; his neck open with a dozen bites and his cheekbones exposed, pink tongue wagging in a mouth of vampiric-looking sharpened teeth that hadn't been there before.

He lunged and grabbed onto the lowest rung of the ladder just before it was carried beyond his reach.

The captain was too many rungs above to pry his former crewmate loose. "Let go, Malcolm! Stay dead!" *Or undead. Damn it, how fast did that transformation happen?*

Malcolm tightened his grip, and even more so, his resolve. In a blind fury, a tunnel vision rage that concentrated his every molecule onto a single task, he held onto that ladder as if it were nothing less than life itself.

The aircraft drew out the remaining length of ladder until Whittaker and Malcolm were lifted along with it. The captain could see but not hear the pilot screaming at him to do something while he pointed down at Malcolm. But there was nothing the captain could do. He was worried enough about his own life at the moment, for below, the horde had arrived. As they waited for the ship to crunch into the pier, which was only seconds away, they looked up, hungrily, hoping maybe that Malcolm would shake the ladder loose and drop Whittaker into their midst.

The chopper dipped with the weight, then flew sideways along with the tanker's motion.

The first zombies, arms outstretched in eager anticipation of a long overdue feeding, crowded under Malcolm, who was now suspended a few feet in the air on the ladder. The helicopter stuttered then dropped when a zombie leapt high, grabbed Malcolm's ankle and hung on. Whittaker screamed as he looked down and saw the impossible: not only had Malcolm locked on, climbing even, but another zombie had jumped and caught Malcolm's ankle, and then—others were leaping, connecting, and holding.

They're making their own goddamned ladder!

Whittaker yelled to the pilot and climbed faster. *Got to get inside, kick off the ladder and all this weight and fly off to safe—*

Unfortunately, the pilot and the other crewman had reached the same conclusion, along with the certainty that they wouldn't last the five seconds it would take for Whittaker to finish his ascent.

"Sorry!" the crewman inside the chopper called out as he worked the ladder's fastening mechanism.

"No, wait!" Whittaker climbed, reaching for the top, for the crewman, even as he mistakenly took a precious second away from his task to look down. He saw the makeshift zombie ladder, and Malcolm's grinning eyes as he served as the anchor—and two crazy-fast corpses scampering up the bodies of the others, stepping on Malcolm's head, then leaping up the rungs. They closed the distance fast to Whittaker, who only had an instant to scream before he felt weightless.

The ladder split and fell free from the chopper, which ascended in a rush of wind and mercifully loud rotor noise.

Loud enough even to drown out his screams as he fell thirty feet to just miss the edge of the deck, to land on his back on the choppy, frothy water.

But the soft landing didn't matter. Seven zombies, including Malcolm, fell with him. On top of him, under him. They landed and sunk, all in one roiling pile, all of them biting and chomping and rending like sharks to a bleeding, helpless, drowning prey.

The last thing he heard, muffled and echoing in the underwater depths, was the sound of his former vessel crunching into the pier, where the rest of the zombie army—and the monstrous dreadnought—would be released onto the mainland.

Part 2: Patient 0

13.

Langley, Virginia

The fact that the CDC maintained an outpost inside the CIA's headquarters was one that was little known, and yet, it made great sense. With the advent of bio-weapons, and with biological warfare on the rise, coordination between the two agencies had been increasingly necessary.

Alex and Elsa Ramirez found themselves escorted by a pair of armed U.S. soldiers along with a contingent of hazmat specialists into a windowless conference room. Ergonomic chairs surrounded a wooden table wired for communications over a slate gray, thin carpet.

A trio of upper echelon CDC division managers were already seated at the table, a battery of electronic devices spread out before them including smartphones, tablets and notebook computers. Alex didn't care. What mattered now was that his mom was finally okay. After all these years of suffering, the uncertainty, the stress of ineffective treatments, at last she was beginning to show real improvement. Nothing could spoil that, not even a sterile debriefing environment with a bunch of government drones.

Yet, as he watched his mother slip into a seat, he knew that something wasn't quite right. That place where they'd had to escape at gunpoint...the improbability of it all....he wished he could understand it better, to make certain that she was really okay. He seated himself directly across from her so that he could look at her closely. The lighting was bright, more than sufficient to conduct a visual examination of her features, which he did while the officials looked on in silence, aware of what he was doing.

Her eyes had not yellowed or taken on the vacant, distracted look like those infected with the zombie agent had. They appeared her same vibrant blue, and yet while they seemed healthy, they also looked somehow…different. Not something he could put his finger on, though, only a vague feeling that her eyes were not quite the same. Perhaps he was mistaken, he thought, turning his attention to her skin.

It, too, lacked the characteristics he feared he might find. No sickly gray pallor or yellowish streaks. No breaks in the skin oozing bodily fluids. Nothing unusual at all, just his mom's pale skin, unbroken and unblemished.

Alex hated that she had to be here, methodically scrutinized like this after so much time away, but he was sure that once they established that she was free of the prions she would be free to go. Even if she had been somehow infected at the Grenada facility, she should have been symptomatic by now.

"It's okay, Alex. I'm fine."

He eyed her dubiously.

"I feel great, really."

"Mom, bear with me for a minute, okay? I need to try and understand what's happening based on my experiences from Adranos Island. To do that I need to ask you some questions." They had given him the list of questions after he had argued she might be more amenable to his asking them than a bunch of nameless others. "It won't take long…okay?"

"Okay, son." She smiled lovingly at him.

The CDC brass exchanged quick glances and then Alex began questioning his mother, for her own sake, and that of society at large.

"Mom, I know these questions may seem silly, but this is…for the record." He glanced at the trio of CDC men at the end of the table.

"That's fine, honey. I understand."

Alex took a deep breath and began. "Once you got to the Grenada facility, did you ever leave until I got there?"

She shook her head. "I was there the whole time. They wouldn't let me go anywhere, as you saw, and I was in no condition to try. I suspect that even if I did, I would have been politely but forcefully returned to my quarters."

Alex nodded. "While you were there, what kind of treatments did they give you? Drugs? Surgeries?"

"There were drugs, antibiotics mostly is what they told me, but no surgeries. They did use a different type of treatment on me, though, one I wasn't expecting."

"Oh? Like what?"

"Like psychotherapy."

Alex appeared confused. He looked down at the CDC guys, who were paying close attention. "Is that the same as just...*therapy*?"

The CDC guys nodded silently. His Mom shrugged. Alex went on.

"So they were asking you personal questions and stuff? Showing you ink blots?"

Elsa smiled patiently. "I didn't get a Rorschach Test, but yes, they engaged me in sessions where they..." She paused as she recalled her memories. "They didn't ask me questions so much as they...I don't know, it's silly, I guess."

Alex shook his head. "No, no, no, it's not silly, Mom. What did they say to you?"

"They were sort of...*hypnotizing* me, I guess, for lack of a better word." She ended the sentence with a girly giggle that she licked her lips at the end of. At this, the CDC professionals stopped their smartphone pecking and eyed one another intensely.

Alex decided to get on with it. The sooner whatever was going to be the result of this meeting happened, the sooner he and his mom could get out of here.

"You mean like, *you are getting sleeeeepy*, kind of stuff, dangling a watch in front of your face?"

She licked her lips again while she remembered. "It was more like a lot of repetitive statements, spoken to me in soft, soothing tones. I thought it was more like meditation therapy, biofeedback or something like that. Relaxing words and ambient music."

"Do you remember any of the statements?"

"They told me I wouldn't be able to remember any of them, but one time I decided not to take the pills they gave me beforehand. I put them into my mouth along with the cup of water they gave me, but I didn't swallow them. I spit them out a couple minutes later when I pretended to sneeze into a Kleenex."

"Why didn't you want to take them?"

"They had nothing to do with my antibiotics or preventing the prion infection. I knew it had to do with the hypnosis stuff and so I wanted to see if I could remember better if I didn't take the pills first."

"And could you?"

She nodded slowly, eyes narrowing. "They would say things like, 'You will follow the commands when you receive them,' or maybe, 'The new sensations you will feel in your head are normal and good for you. Do not fight them...' Over and over and over for I don't even know how long. They never had any clocks on the wall and they confiscated my watch and phone upon arrival."

Alex looked over at the CDC contingent, all three of whom stared at his mother with rapt attention, and suddenly he was sick of it all. This was outrageous. His mother had been through a traumatic experience. Simply having cancer in the first place was bad enough, but then she had undergone some hyper-experimental medical procedure out of country to boot? There was nothing more he needed to learn here. He stood up and stared directly into one of the low profile dome cameras he'd noticed recessed into the ceiling. He figured it was just a regular videoconference camera. This was the lion's den for the CIA, after all, and if they wanted to put cameras in here that were undetectable to the human eye, he was sure they could do it. Maybe they did do it. He didn't know and he didn't care. He just wanted to get his point across, so he shouted it at the top of his lungs.

"She does *not* have the virus, or the prion, or whatever the hell it is! I've seen the symptoms, seen them dozens of times on Adranos, and this..." he pointed dramatically at his mother. "...Is. Not. It!"

His mother smiled at Alex and licked her lips again, this time accompanying the action with a small yet perceptible nod of the head. Alex wanted to tell his mother to stop doing that, if this was her idea of a joke it wasn't funny in the slightest, but he didn't want to call attention to it in case it had gone unnoticed by the

CDC and all the other invisible flies on the wall in here. He just wanted to get her out of here, to take her home.

"How was she cured, Alex? That's all we're trying to find out." The voice startled him, not because of the words it carried, or the fact that it came from a speaker somewhere on the table, but because of who it belonged to.

Veronica. She sounded calm, matter-of-fact. He had no reason to doubt her. She continued.

"Go ahead and take a break. You've given us good information. We have a blood sample from Elsa that technicians are analyzing now. Just give us a few more minutes, Alex. I'll be in shortly with the test results."

Alex thanked Veronica and immediately the CDC men began conversing in near-whispered tones, clearly not wanting Alex or his mother to hear what was being said. After a few seconds, they stood and told Alex they'd be in the next room, that he and his mom should feel free to "catch up on things."

Alex waited until they walked out of the room and the door had closed behind them to start talking, even though he supposed they were being monitored, probably even recorded in here. They were as alone as they were going to be though, so he reached across the table and took his mother's hand. And her skin felt different. He hadn't thought to actually feel her skin earlier, he had only looked at it. But holding it now, it felt...*you know the word, admit it...it feels slightly...just a little bit...scaly.*

He wasn't sure if his mind was playing tricks on him, like how he'd heard that if you imagined things for long enough they would start to seem real even though they weren't. He clasped her hand with his other hand, just to refresh the tactile stimulation and hopefully trigger a new sensation, one of normal, smooth human female skin. But it still had that hint of scaliness.

Yet she looked...*be honest*...she looked good for someone who had until very recently been in the grips of advanced stage cancer. But deep down a nagging worry needled his consciousness. What if the cancer wasn't responsible for how she looked now? What if she had been cured, but somehow altered in the process? She had been taken, after all, to some foreign facility where FDA laws may very well not apply. He imagined a coterie of overzealous researchers guinea-pigging his mom to death in some sterile laboratory...and then bringing her back. Maybe he'd seen *Pet Sematary* too many times as a kid, but even as she talked to him now, asking him if he remembered that cottage where they went on vacation twenty years ago, but without waiting for an answer, something just seemed *off* about her.

He decided to redirect the conversation. She seemed to be a little more normal when he'd been questioning her. Or was that because she'd known that to exhibit symptoms of whatever it was she had in the presence of the CDC would be detrimental to her freedom, and now that they were no longer staring her directly in the face she felt like she could let her guard down a little? Or maybe she *had to* let her guard down, as if it had taken all of her limited reserves of energy to pull off the charade.

"Mom? Let me ask you about Dad, please. I know you didn't get to say goodbye. I didn't either, well...not really, not the way I would have liked, but at least I did have some last *words* with him." He flashed on the insect larvae pouring from his father's mouth during his final moments on that godforsaken island, how they had impeded his speech, and he shuddered involuntarily. If his mother noticed the movement, she didn't say anything. "You didn't get that chance."

Elsa smiled that slightly vacant expression again. "I'm at peace with your father."

Alex thought about this for a few seconds. She had to be just saying that not to make him feel bad. "That's good. I know he would have wanted to say goodbye to you. It's terrible he didn't get that chance. He told me on the ship in Antarctica that he wished I would call and visit you more."

Elsa Ramirez suddenly tensed, her expression going slack, eyes blank, one of her hands gripping the edge of the conference table.

"You never should have let that asshole tell you what to do. I never did, that's for fucking sure."

Alex sat there, not even breathing as he stared at his mother. He'd never heard her talk like this before, ever. He wanted to ask her if she was all right, or maybe if there was something that happened in the past he didn't know about, but "Mom?" was all that came out.

"He can rot in goddamned Hell for all I care."

Again, Alex flashed on his father's diseased mouth and reptilian teeth, the maggots and the Herculean effort he'd required to fumble out his last words.

Alex stood, his chair toppling onto the floor. "Mom! Stop talking like that!"

"Or what?" Elsa Ramirez leaned forward over the table.

Alex was speechless.

"What's my little Alex going do about it? Nothing, that's what. 'Cuz you're a pussy, son, just like you always were. Can't do shit."

He stared, incredulous, for another moment, then backed away. "That's it. I'm out of here." He turned and walked around the fallen chair, speaking as he went. "I went through a lot of trouble to come here to try and help you, and this is how you thank me?"

As he rounded the chair and began walking toward the door, he got another look at his mother's face. Her eyes were definitely yellowish now. Not a faint, jaundiced kind of yellow, but a crisp, electric yellow, and not across the entire orb but only part of the iris. It was weird. He could swear her eyes weren't like that *before...before...before* all this happened when everything was normal. He wanted to go back to that period in his life, but there was no time for that kind of nostalgic longing now, because Now was obviously so very different from Then, when the woman sitting across from him made him chocolate chip cookies and read him stories and tucked him into bed at night. Now she was cursing and leering at him in a CDC/CIA hybrid facility with yellow eyes, and...

And jumping up on the table! She leapt, lips parted in a feral, instinctive gesture. Alex sidestepped her attack and she landed on two feet against the wall, then sprang off with cat-like speed. He stepped forward. In an ordinary fight, his next move would have been to duck under the wild attack and try to get a punch in hard to her face and then maybe pin her to the floor as she dropped. But even as he interlaced the fingers of his two hands, one in front of the other to deliver a hammer blow, he knew he wouldn't be able to do it.

Gone-crazy freak or not, she was still his mother, the one who had brought him into this world, as unpleasant as that world had become. He could not will himself to physically harm her, so he ducked out of the way, spun and raced toward the door. He reached it and flung it open.

Two soldiers were posted immediately outside, and they both spun, caught off guard at his wild appearance. He grabbed the doorknob and slammed the door shut behind him, leaning against it as something crushed into it from the other side.

"What the hell was that?" one of them asked.

"The CDC guys?" Alex hissed. "Where are they?" He had questions for them. Boy, did he ever.

One of the soldiers spoke softly into a speaker microphone mounted on his shoulder. As he did so, his associate tapped him on the arm and pointed at the window into the room, where Elsa Ramirez had backed up, then raced lightning-fast toward the door. It burst open, frame shattered in her wake.

She bull-rushed the guards, reaching Alex first but shoving him out of the way. One of the guards moved for his weapon but the pistol hung up on the holster catch as he tried to remove it and she knocked his hand away. The other soldier, thinking he'd have an easy time with this old woman, crazy as she may be, pinned her against the wall. She wryly slid under his grasp, shoved him aside with surprising strength.

"Jesus! Get her down!" the soldier who had tried to calm her said. Both soldiers jumped on her but she was like a Tasmanian Devil, a whirlwind of chaotic thrashing, flailing and random movement that was impossible to stop.

"She on meth?" one of the soldiers gasped, staring up at Alex from his position on the floor, where he'd been knocked to his back.

"No! Just hold her!"

Elsa wriggled a hand free and then struck—jamming a narrow index finger with a huge elongated nail into one of the soldiers' eyes. He promptly cried out, shrieking in agony and clutching his bleeding eye socket as Elsa then turned her fury onto the military man who already lay on his back. Alex was there in a second, leaning in to break it up, pulling his mother's head back as her mouth was open, jaws snapping at the air with a vulgar sucking sound. Alex stood up, shoved her back, then realized too late that he had let himself get much too close.

She turned and made eye contact with him and blinked—once, twice. Alex noticed that those eyes suddenly shifted and seemed to look more normal now. A little yellow, but not so much.

"Love you, son," his mother rasped, and then she coughed, a guttural, violent, bloody sound. She shuddered, and as the guard on the ground got up, freeing his weapon, she took off, running smoothly down the hall. The three men wearing suits who had been inside the room came skidding around a corner, sound-suppressed pistols drawn. Apparently they'd been monitoring the situation as it unfolded. They glanced at the guard with the hole in his eye, whose mouth was moving but with no sound coming out, and then at Alex, who was way beyond a mere loss for words, half-standing-half-kneeling, completely dumbfounded by the sudden chain of events.

One of the CDC guys said, "Sector 7 Hallway, heading East," into a radio and Alex heard the footfalls of multiple men come running from a hallway off to his right. Beneath him, the penned guard gasped, shuddered and went still.

His mother had killed someone, and—Alex had to finally accept—was most certainly infected, and free around this facility.

That fact somehow disturbed him less than the sudden suspicion that her release from Grenada, complete with the staged guard's reactions, had been planned from the beginning.

Planned to get him to bring her here.

He shuddered and ran, chasing after the men. Chasing after her.

14.

Veronica left the control room in a rush. Where was her backup? Where was the support?

Alarms were going off everywhere, sounding like echoes from air raid sirens, as if enemy bombers were incoming and everyone had to flee to shelters. However, she wasn't fleeing. Not a chance. Instead, she listened, focusing on the loudest source of commotion. The next hallway over, where she heard trampling feet, shouts and—gunfire!

She drew her 9mm and raced around a corner to find two servicemen in a bloody heap on the floor, with three more guards standing around them, one reaching down to check for a pulse.

"Stop!" Veronica yelled, aiming and trying to get a lock on the corpse's skull. "Step away from them!"

The would-be helper glanced back, fingers on the dead man's neck—just as its eyes opened. Yellow eyes, Veronica saw.

"Down!"

Too late, the dead man-turned-zombie lurched up, grabbed the living man's neck and turned him around as he locked his jaws on the man's neck. His shocked eyes locked on Veronica's and froze her for a moment, a moment that in hindsight didn't matter. Once bitten…

They were both goners, and Veronica hastened their end. Two shots: the twitching, dying man in the center of his forehead, the zombie through its right temple. The two other soldiers backed up, drawing their guns, aiming at Veronica, shocked and in utter confusion, with the alarms, the gunfire and the sight of their friends just put down with headshots.

Veronica raised her arms, but then pointed to the other dead man *(was he killed by Elsa as well? Had to be… oh God, how did they let this happen? And where was Alex?)* The thought drove an ice stake through her heart, but action called her back to the present. She dropped, aimed and fired low, just missing the head of the other zombie, clipping its shoulder. About to bite one of the soldiers, his friend reacted faster, or by sheer instinct—and drove the butt of his automatic rifle down against the thing's head, knocking it back, dazed.

Then both men aimed their guns at the thrashing creature as Veronica ran up between them, gun outstretched.

"Don't waste time questioning your vision." She fired, blasting a hole in the zombie's skull just as it was about to lunge at her. With just a glance back at the men, she ran ahead, toward the commotion. "Come on, now you know what to do. Anyone bitten who looks dead…"

"…isn't," said one of the soldiers, shaking his head as he watched the body missing half its head slump to the floor.

#

Veronica rounded the corner, into the lobby and skidded to a halt. How had it gotten this far already? Two agents in plainclothes—a man and a woman, nerdy types from level three, she realized—had been infected and changed. They were charging the front desk where two armed guards with a no-nonsense attitude didn't think twice, but cut down the attackers.

Good, Veronica thought, seeing them go for headshots. *Word's finally out, and they believe my briefing.*

The area safe, more agents and soldiers emerged from hallways and around cover.

"Lobby secure," one agent in a black suit spoke into his Bluetooth. Veronica, taking a breath, was about to agree—when a shadow fell over the lobby, something blocking out the sun from the western set of windows on the second level.

Something large, something…

"Get down!" she screamed, running for cover—the nearest pillar.

An explosion of glass, tortured metal and concrete bursting apart. Shards rained down on the soldiers and agents, trying to dodge and flee the gray-leathery thing that had flown right into the building.

Veronica would have thought it a small plane at first, except for the stench.

The horrid, fetid stench of something that should have been dead millions of years ago.

Something that awkwardly careened off a pillar, shattering off a huge chunk of masonry, then flapping and rolling and gripping the third level landing with its giant claws...

It opened its beak. Its hideously vacant and remorseless eyes seemed to seek out Veronica's, to root her to the spot, even as it regurgitated its payload.

Two human figures spilled from it gullet, tumbling, thrashing and alighting onto the marble floor beneath—

—where they promptly shook off the fall, got up, chose targets, and ran...

#

She couldn't even get a shot off before the huge black shape fell to the floor, crashed and heaved itself up, spreading its wings and rearing back its enormous head. Pockets of flesh hung off the creature, as its eyes—empty, hideous, famished—continued to stare hungrily at Veronica.

The fear she felt now, confined in this building, surrounded by other zombies and screaming colleagues, was even more acute than being down in the cargo hold of the *Hammond* with the chained *T.rex...*

This thing was vile, unearthly and alien in a different way, as if its malice and brooding terror came not from animalistic nature, but from sheer evil itself—from the very nature of evil.

The utter weight of those eyes, the slavering bloody ooze dripping from its beak, and the enormous wingspan, all served to freeze her in her tracks like susceptible prey.

She was a goner.

Except in the next instant, as the pterodactyl reared back and was about to launch upon her, a strafing run of bullets—armor piercing 50-caliber rounds—tore through its right side, from shoulder to skull. Veronica watched in awe as the rounds fired from a second story turret and an M2 machine gun raked the undead creature up and down and sideways, shredding its skin and bone as it would a tank or armored vehicle.

The pterodactyl issued a baneful shrieking as it flapped and tried to cover its head with its wings—that were subsequently obliterated, and then it lifted its beak and made one last attempt to snap at its unseen attackers. After that, another salvo bored holes through its carapace, shattering its skull and blasting its brain stem into gory shreds.

Its neck almost completely severed, it flopped awkwardly backward and lay flat, with its wings spread out in tatters. Smoke rose from its bullet-ridden body.

The gun went silent as Veronica looked up, now with the sun back and streaming through the broken window, where she could just make out the machine gunner running from the turret toward the stairs and down to join the closer fighting below.

She recognized the man as he appeared on the lower landing. Recognized him from the briefing about the aircraft carrier's attack. He was a pilot, and Alex's escort, and must have been finishing his debrief here as well when the assault began.

Clear-thinker, she thought proudly. Major Casey Remington rounded the pillar just as Veronica leapt over the ptero's twitching tail. They both had their sidearms out, taking aim at the pair of zombies engaged with unarmed CIA agents trying to keep them at bay with a fire extinguisher.

Two shots, each firing simultaneously, and the two zombies fell, backs of their skulls blown out.

"Nice shooting," Remington said to her.

"You too, and thanks." She nodded back to the twice-dead flying dinosaur. "Was that three of those birds you've killed now?"

He nodded. "By my count. Although it's getting easier. And thanks to you and your briefing. Head shots…"

She nodded, then glanced around, listening. "Is that all of them?"

More gunfire erupted down the western hallway, followed by screams.

"Damn it, they've gotten into the building."

"Go," Remington said. "Help where you can, I have other orders."

"What orders?"

"I've got to get into the air and protect the harbor, and… do what I can from the air." He gave the pterodactyl a wide berth, but lingered with a look of grudging awe and respect, then turned back to her. "I have a feeling we'll meet again."

She met his look and saw the fear lodged there, the same almost resigned acceptance one would expect seeing a tidal wave heading toward an unprotected beach. She hoped it wasn't true, but thought: *maybe all we can do is hang on and wait for the aftermath.*

As he ran off, a new round of gunfire echoed from the eastern hallway. Veronica froze, undecided. The lobby was empty but for the dead dinosaur and the corpses with their heads shot up. She hesitated, unsure in which direction to run and provide aid, but then heard screams and shouts outside, as well as a roaring and something unearthly rumbling in the streets. She saw the broken front entrance and wondered for a moment if the best spot for her might actually be at the turret upstairs, guarding the entrance and shooting anything that shambled inside. They had to protect this intelligence center. Who knows what was happening out there, but inside, they had access to worldwide communications, an arsenal, a bunker and could hold out and direct the outside forces if need be.

However, if those screams from the other hallways were any indication, Langley's interior was far from secure. Whoever planned all this—and did she even have to wonder—knew what they were doing, attacking it first as a high priority target.

Then she shuddered, thinking of the planning, and what she would have done if she were on the other side. What other targets would have been selected, and what other battles were raging right now?

In the midst of such questions, her phone rang.

It was Nesmith. She was wanted in the control room, mission of vital importance. She couldn't hear everything through the gunfire, but it sounded like they needed her to get to Atlanta, where there just might be a key to stopping all this.

15.

CDC Headquarters, Atlanta

Arcadia was close to finding a synthesis that actually made sense, nowhere near to a complete understanding of what this thing was, but she was running a program to break down Xander's complicated algorithms and unravel the protein inhibitors to get at what this prion could do.

She also had to see what this invasive agent couldn't do. What it couldn't attack, break down, control and devour. In the midst of all this research and focus, she almost didn't hear the commotion until the office had broken out into complete chaos. Other researchers and doctors surrounded computer screens and TV monitors at first, pointing with shaking hands, then looks of fear, a bustling of activity, people scrambling for their cell phones.

Arcadia stood up, making to head out of her office, when her laptop screen flashed to a media app they all had running in the background. *Look away,* she told herself, just don't look. Go out there, and maybe it'll be something else, something normal like another mass shooting—as unfortunately 'normal' that has become in this day and age. The screen changed and of course, she couldn't look away. Not from the multiple angles and raw footage of the impossible:

Dinosaurs, things out of B-movies, except with greater realism and terror, these things—some she recognized, others were different, like those pale, swift creatures with crown-like appendages.

The cameras were shaky—maybe hand-held phones and video apps—again in this day, all too popular. This was CNN, but she knew they would all be carrying more of the same, and after the initial certainty that this had to be a hoax or the ultimate prank, terror would be sweeping the country, gripping it. The world even.

She sat back down, mesmerized. The horror, the devastation...and the transformations. She watched, and quickly the brutality and the violence and sheer insanity of it all gave way to a scientist's interest. Her curiosity and observational nature took over. She studied the ferocity of the zombie attacks, the movements of the dinosaurs, the rising of the corpses after attack, and most importantly…the means of transfer.

The prions.

In her mind she saw the protein structures, the way they reacted to and conquered their surrounding cells.

She saw the human victims on these videos. Bitten by other infected humans. Bitten—but surprisingly not eaten completely—by the dinosaurs. It was as if the raging attackers knew they had to leave enough of the flesh and muscle (and teeth) to keep the body alive, to be able to reproduce in the only way they could.

A few more minutes, and she was still riveted, studying details and picking up knowledge most of the viewers likely missed. Scenes shifted, cities changed, but it was all the same. Whether it was Miami or Charlotte or Baltimore… Or the current scene—from Atlanta itself, where something of incredible size, with a huge brontosaurus-like neck, lumbered away from a flatbed 18-wheeler, crushing townhomes, restaurants, people and everything in its wake. It reminded her superficially of a video she'd once seen of an escaped circus elephant rampaging through city streets until it had to be stopped by police with shotguns, only this was so much worse, orders of magnitude worse.

Oh god.

That brought her back, and now she realized what the commotion was all about in her office.

Just then, all the CDC breach alarms went off. The panic buttons had been hit.

They were here.

#

"Levels four through six secure."

Arcadia listened with only some minor fraction of her attention. She implicitly understood that, at least for the moment, she and her colleagues were safe here, and she imagined that should the building stability or facility in total be threatened, they could take a secure elevator non-stop down to the bunker-level and the highest degree of security, the underground level where all the truly dangerous chemicals and bio-threats were kept behind multiple firewall and security precautions.

For now, she hoped the security measures—including external window sealing, multiple locked entry points and reinforced walls, would hold.

Unless something like that thing with the enormous neck comes this way...what could stop that short of a guided missile?

She shuddered, put it out of her mind and focused on the incoming communication.

Forget for a moment the chaos reigning outside, the prehistoric creatures attacking the city like Godzilla on steroids.

The president was calling.

16.

Veronica listened, but understood only about a third of what the CDC Director said—and she had the sneaking suspicion that even that was half more than the president himself comprehended. She had to give him the benefit of the doubt though, as his attention was absorbed in a million other directions: his country under attack, the capital itself in serious danger. Civilization itself seemed to be hanging in the balance.

She could hear the planes overhead, the sonic booms, bombs and gunfire, and she shuddered with each thudding that shook the building and rattled dust over her. The screen ahead, however, was crystal clear, the president on the left, the CDC Director of Pathogen Research on the right.

They both looked like hell, but Arcadia's eyes at least held a promise of hope.

"Agent Winters," the president said, as he winced, looking up and over his shoulder.

"Sir, are you secure?"

"Underground and behind multiple walls of steel? I sure hope so, but there won't be a nation left to govern if we can't stop this thing. If Dr. Grey's infection projections are true, and we can't end this here and now…"

Arcadia shook her head. "If it was just Atlanta, or just Baltimore? Maybe. You could block all the roads, secure the city, even…do the unthinkable and nuke the area."

The president closed his eyes for a moment, then opened them again. They looked hardened and pained. "Scary as that option is, I wish it were on the table. But we have no choice at all. As she says, with six cities and counting under attack, we'll never have the resources."

"Then why am I here?" Veronica asked. *And why am I here? Surely these two should be spending their precious time on other alternatives.*

The president sighed and settled his attention on her. "We'll do our best in the air and with ground troops to contain this, repel the…things and control the spread of the infection, and even if we

fail, there are secure locations around the country. Even now..."
He rubbed his eyes.

Was he about to tell her what she had already guessed? There
were shadow government sites, bunkers in secure locations around
the country, possibly NORAD in Cheyenne Mountain, Colorado,
among others, where an alternate cabinet and leadership structure
stood ready to take control should Washington fall. She knew all
about it in the wake of the 9-11 attacks, and how close we had
come to another plane knocking out the White House and the
Pentagon.

"Contingencies are in effect," the president said, echoing her
thoughts, "but what Dr. Grey has brought to my attention is
something that may be a silver bullet, a long shot, but hope
nonetheless."

"And it concerns you," Arcadia Grey said to Veronica, "since it
came from Xander Dyson."

Veronica's breath froze. She tried not to show a reaction, but
she knew something about Xander might come up on this call if it
involved the CDC Director. Arcadia Grey was Dyson's girlfriend
for a time, it was all in the file, and Veronica knew everything
about the man, every aspect of his past, every family member,
friend, lover and acquaintance. She had left no stone unturned, but
also she had a tremendous amount of respect for Dr. Grey. She
did, after all, dump the bastard and then reveal everything she
could about him to the FBI and CIA. She had been mortified by
the level of his sadism and the misuse of his talents in the name of
some misbegotten undertaking.

Still, discussing Dyson at all was painful for Veronica. He had
killed her fiancée, after all, and now...

"I'm sorry, Agent Winters." Dr. Grey appeared solemn and
pale. She shook her head slowly. "I wish I could have stopped
Dyson before...before he hurt anyone."

"Thank you, but..."

"I'm not sure if you were aware of this, but while you were on
that island, when it became clear to him that DeKirk was going to
sell him out and steal his science, Dyson worked on something
that might just be the key we need to reverse all this."

Veronica tried to think of a question, some response to make any kind of sense out of what she had just been told. "Are you sure? Alex and I...when we were in that facility, it looked like Xander Dyson was bluffing while he was communicating with DeKirk. He claimed he had a 'failsafe' just at the time needed it to save his ass."

"I thought of that, too," the president said, "but Dr. Grey assures me she's checked the science, the biology."

"It's sound," Arcadia said. "It's not complete though, not totally, but it's close. Dyson knew it, knew if he sent me what he had, that I could finish the work, see how the elements all fit and put the rest of the jigsaw together. I would realize his theory was correct. There's a way to use the prions' own transfer mechanisms against them. There's a way to control them, first off—"

"—which is probably what DeKirk took from Dyson," the president added, "and why these mindless creatures seem to be acting with more intelligence than they should have." He sighed. "Not that I'm a goddamned dinosaur expert, but the fact that these things with little more than bird brains are strategically dropping off payloads, running elaborate diversions and hitting key targets all speaks to something—or someone—controlling them."

Dr. Grey nodded. "Without getting into the complexities of the science, the similarities to group consciousness, migratory patterns and pack mentality, there's something even beyond that that these things share..."

"No time, doctor."

"Right. Sorry." Arcadia glanced down, then winced at some noise in the background.

"Is it still secure there?" Veronica asked.

"For the moment," Arcadia responded, "but we don't know how much longer. There was something coming up from the south, something big, saw it on the news, transported by a huge truck."

"We don't know what its target is," the president said, "but we're not taking any chances. The National Guard has been mobilized."

Dr. Grey leaned closer so Veronica could see the red in her eyes, the lines around her cheekbones and her thin lips. She wondered if, a lifetime ago, under different circumstances, she and Xander Dyson could have had a normal life. Dinner parties, kids, family outings...

"I've uploaded everything I have so far on the research. Sharing it with your lab there at Langley."

"That's enough for now," the president said. "We're not sure of DeKirk's reach, or what he can tap into, but we don't want to tip our hand in any way if this can help. So no word on the Dyson research or this failsafe to anyone. In the meantime, Agent Winters?"

"Yes sir?"

"I need you to perform an extraction."

"Sir?"

"Dr. Grey is too valuable to leave unprotected, and...with what we can extrapolate from the tactics and behavior of this army of things...the CDC is a prime target."

"I agree, sir," Veronica said nervously. "So send in the National Guard to get her out of there, to a secure location..."

She stopped as he was shaking his head. "You don't understand. All forces are already engaged, or were pulled to other strategic sites to engage the enemy. They would take too long to redirect, and with these things and the way they spread the infection, less is more."

Veronica swallowed hard. She met Arcadia's eyes.

"I'm sorry," Dr. Grey said. "I know I'm probably the last person you want to spend your time saving, and you must have a hundred questions about why I didn't do more to stop my former boyfriend, but I just hope you'll understand—"

Veronica's tone was icy. "I do. You might be our only hope."

"Exactly what I was going to say," the president added, then glanced nervously to something on another screen on his end. "Going to have to cut this short. You two work out the logistics, and Agent Winters, there's a pilot waiting at Andrews. Take anyone else you need, but limit it to one or two more. Get in, extract Dr. Grey and any research materials she needs, and get back in the air. You'll be heading to Colorado."

Veronica nodded. Washington might soon be lost. They were already considering the backup plans, and if that was so, everything had gone to shit a hell of a lot faster than she imagined. She wondered if the alternate shadow government waited in Colorado or if that was too obvious. NORAD could be controlled by the shadow leaders after power was transferred, but it was best done from a more remote location. She just wondered where...

She nodded, and as the president—looking grim and pale—disappeared from the screen, Veronica turned her attention to Dr. Grey.

"I'm sorry," the CDC Director said again.

"Don't be." She met her gaze, and they held it together—a look of shared loss, pain and regret. Veronica finally broke the silence.

"When you think about it, we have to be thankful now we never stopped Dyson, because if not for him, I guess we wouldn't have any hope right now."

"I hate to admit it, but you're right. He was a bastard, but a goddamned genius."

Veronica matched her thin smile. "Okay, tell me about the CDC headquarters, and let's come up with a quick plan for extraction. I'll be there in under two hours unless we hit a snag."

"Like a dinosaur roadblock?"

"Don't even joke. Can you survive until then?"

Dr. Grey nodded. "Can you?"

17.

CIA Special Agent Debbie Harris, after leaving the last in a series of briefings—quite possibly the last ever from this president—headed to the roof. She had to make a call on the secure satellite phone, but it was too risky inside the building, and likely jammed.

She had to reach DeKirk and warn him. The CDC...they had something. She'd only overheard bits of the details, but a mission had just been green-lighted. Top priority extraction of someone or some information down there. Too urgent to share over conventional channels. She knew DeKirk was concerned about the CDC, but he didn't assign it high enough value to merit a first-wave strike.

This was why he had chosen her, why she'd been on his payroll for years, doing nothing except listening. Sure, she occasionally fed his associates information on the CIA manhunt or the investigation into his finances, but that was nothing new for him—he had it covered and was well protected. Her updates had probably just served as entertainment and to confirm how far ahead of his hunters he remained.

This, however, he hadn't foreseen. It was still a long shot, but Agent Harris wasn't taking any chances. If the president himself thought this was the highest priority, she had to convey it to DeKirk, and fast.

Rounding a corner, phone in hand, she gingerly stepped past a pair of bodies—guards with nasty bites in their necks and bullet holes in their skulls. She choked back an involuntary rise of bile, then looked up at the nearest full-wall length window as an F/A-18 fighter jet tore across her view. She heard high-caliber machine gun fire from somewhere below, and explosions from outside while she approached the elevator bank, pressed the UP button and continued to stare at the scene outside.

Trails of smoke rising from city streets. Buildings on fire. Giant bird-like shapes in the air, swooping down on motorists and into the midst of crowds. Chased by numerous planes, aerial battles occurred in a surreal, almost theatrical display as more fireballs rocked the city.

She felt detached, beyond it all. Didn't know whether to smile or choke back revulsion. She had been a part of all this, at first an unwilling part as DeKirk had kidnapped her daughter. That had only been a first step, a bluff, in essence. He'd let her go long before Harris knew about it because by then, he had her. She had divulged national security secrets, a treasonous sin punishable by death. There was nowhere for her to run, and she was his. She had to continue to serve in any way he wanted.

Still, there were rewards. He knew how to offer incentives as well as threats.

A new world order was coming, a grand feast, and those who had proven themselves would earn a place at the table.

Harris gripped the phone tighter and turned away from the horror outside, praying that the end would come swiftly for all those out there who woke up this morning thinking it would just be another day.

She thought of her daughter and prayed that she took her mother's advice and got to Alaska, the safe zone she had been promised would remain as such...but there was no time to think about her now.

The call. The CDC mission. She had to warn DeKirk, and surely this act would seal in her reward for good. Maybe even elevate her position for such loyalty and fast-thinking.

Come on, she thought. *Damn elevator, open already, op—*

The chime sounded and the doors opened. Harris smiled and was about to step in when she recoiled in horror.

The elevator was already occupied.

Three women and a man—torn open in all the wrong places, their flesh and clothes ripped apart and all merged into some unholy mass of crimson and other colors, highlighted by protruding bones, the flesh stripped and gnawed on by the other woman in the cab.

Old, bald. Drenched in blood, with ragged bits of raw meat and muscle stuffed into her mouth, sharp teeth sawing the flesh to bits. Her throat was engorged, the muscles swallowing methodically like a python.

Elsa Ramirez lifted her head slowly, and those eyes, tinted yellowish now and swimming with still-unfulfilled hunger, settled on Harris.

She let out a low, deep sigh. The agent knew the call would not be made, but her reward was nonetheless at hand.

Elsa leapt up in a rage, bloody hands and snapping teeth finding their target.

Harris went down, her neck torn open in mid-scream. The phone sailed out of reach and Elsa went to work on the agent's flesh with unbridled passion and renewed hunger.

18.

Alex fled at the roar of the gunfire, where fighting sounded like it came from all directions. He felt trapped, cornered in a confusing series of hallways and stairs and empty rooms, without backup or support or any other sign of life. He heard snarls and rending noises from inside one room, the door slightly ajar. Peeked in to see a young woman in a smart navy suit straddling over a thrashing man. Under any other circumstances, Alex might have thought something entirely different, but he heard the wild screams, saw blood spraying as she whipped her head back and forth, tearing at the soft flesh under his chin.

Goner, Alex thought, and backed away, easing the door shut.

He wished he had a gun. Didn't even have to be anything fancy at this point. A revolver, even a knife. Anything. He had to find someone with a spare weapon, or find a dead body with one still on it.

There. A pair of legs around the next corner, under a blinking red alarm light. The sound had gone silent, but the pulses continued. As he approached the body, he wondered how much of the facility had fallen. Where was his mother, and was she the cause of it all? He had brought her back here against his better judgment. She was his mother, the only link to a past he had regretfully squandered. Since his return from Antarctica, he had wanted to make things right. Somehow, any way possible. He should have seen the signs, should have known it was too good to be true.

The building shook violently and Alex grabbed the wall for support. *What the hell was that?* He imagined a plane had just been taken down, its wing clipped before it crashed into the base of the CIA building.

Whatever it was, it passed without further destruction. He advanced on the body, coming within yards of the man's feet. Another step, and in the flashing crimson radiance he could make out more of the corpse. Saw a sidearm—still holstered at the belt, under a dark red stain down the front of the guard's shirt.

Then suddenly, swiftly, the body was yanked backwards, almost out of sight. Alex leapt back, stumbled and fell hard, grunting.

Whoever or whatever pulled the guard certainly heard that. Alex froze, unwilling and unable to make a move. If he got up, the sound would alert the thing, and if he stayed still, it would surely round the corner and see him—if it didn't smell him already.

I'm dead, I'm dead, I'm...

He saw the hair first. Bloodstained and grayish-blonde. Actually saw blood dripping off the fine strands before he saw the crazed yellow eyes, the face and neck—with chewed flesh pulled free. He was surprised the head was even still on, with all that damage. Muscles and sinews bitten clean through to the vertebrae. The head lolled to the side, but the jaws still snapped and the tongue circled obscenely through a gash torn from the right cheek.

He recognized the woman from the briefing room. She was Agent Harry or something. Veronica thought she was a bitch, and now...now that bitch had seen him. She leapt over the dead guard who might have been her first meal, and bounded on all fours toward Alex. Her head flopping back on her left shoulder, a horrible hissing sound issued from her throat, rising in pitch.

Alex reared back reflexively, lifted his knees to his chest, and as Agent Harris pounced, his feet caught her in her bony chest. His legs bent back, then pushed hard out, sending her high in the air—

—as gunshots erupted and bullet holes riddled her body from her collarbone up. Her skull split open and splattered the ceiling with gore while she continued her descent and rolled back on the floor, limp and completely dead.

Alex turned around.

Veronica was there, AK-47 in both hands, still aiming down the sights.

"Nice shooting," Alex said.

"Thank you," Veronica replied, lowering the gun, "for the assist. Hated her anyway."

He got up swiftly, walked around Harris, then got to the guard and retrieved the Beretta 9mm just as the corpse started to twitch.

"Damn it, hate when this happens!" He cocked it, thinking Veronica wouldn't get there in time. Aimed, then backed up, keeping his arm straight and level as the body shifted and the zombie sat up, head swiveling, blood still draining from great tears in his throat and shoulders.

The red lights flashed, the body rose, and still he couldn't fire. Not because of the horror of the moment or the fact that this was just a normal guy a few hours ago, but because another figure had entered the hallway.

Stepping out from elevator doors a few yards away, shuffling aimlessly ahead, sniffing the air as if seeking departed prey, or fresh meat, his mother turned her head, and found him.

She licked her blood-stained lips and crimson-chipped teeth, and ran.

#

Alex shifted the gun's aim. Only partially aware of the guard rising up now, getting to his knees, snarling, drooling. He could sense the hunger but despite the proximity of the threat, his brain could only react to the other threat: his mother racing toward him, arms outstretched for a last grisly embrace.

"Mom, no!"

Gunfire behind him, a grunt to his side, along with a sick, splattering sound.

"...not your mom, not her..." came a distant voice.

Alex didn't hear it fully, didn't comprehend. Or perhaps he did, but on some other level altogether.

What he did next, he did not do out of reflex, self-preservation or even mercy.

He did for another reason.

"Love you..." he started to say, but had the words snuffed out as he pulled the trigger.

Three times. Two of the shots missed, the third punctured his mother's forehead and dropped her at his feet.

He stared at the body, face-down. Not twitching, not moving.

So at peace.

He didn't even hear Veronica slide to a stop behind him. Didn't see the gun pointing at the guard, then his mom, then Agent Harris's body, sweeping the hall for other threats.

Didn't feel her touch his shoulder or next, her body pressing against his back then wrapping her arms around his chest.

Didn't hear her whisper apologies in his ear.

He turned away from his mother, sliding fully into Veronica's embrace.

Held her tight in the flashing lights that seemed to pulse in slower increments. Held her until another exterior explosion rocked the building and rained dust and debris on their heads.

"We better move," she said into his ear. Gently. There was no other way. Nothing else to say. She held him close, tense, ready to prevent him from turning around again for another look.

"You did the right the thing," she whispered. "The only thing."

He nodded, feeling a tear slide against her cheek. His or hers, he wasn't sure, but he knew Elsa had found her way into Veronica's heart as well these past few months.

He swallowed hard and nodded. Pulled back and looked into Veronica's eyes. He needed something, some hope to cling to now, something to fight back the terror of what was happening here, and outside—and who knew where else in the world?

"I started this. We…" he glanced over his shoulder despite her attempt to stop him. "We started it."

"No," Veronica objected. "If it wasn't you, it would have been someone or something else. DeKirk had a thousand options for how to release this hell upon the world. He just wanted to get back at you because we did our best back there on that island. But if using your mom hadn't worked, he would have infiltrated the CDC some other way. He was too many steps ahead of all of us."

"So what do we do now? Is there any hope?"

She didn't answer at first, just held his gaze. At length, she nodded.

"Yes. You're coming with me." She broke the embrace, slung the gun over her shoulder and took his free hand.

"Where?"

"Well, first, we're fighting our way out of this building. Then we're going to get to a vehicle, and then race to Andrews Air Force base..."

Alex paled. "Driving? Out in that war zone?"

"Yeah, sounds easy, doesn't it?"

"Then what?"

"Tell you on the way. Come on, move it." She squeezed his hand. "And don't look back again. We have a shot at this, but I need you focused and in control."

Alex took a breath. "I'm with you. I have scores to settle."

"You will." She steered him around the bodies and toward the elevator. "Trust me, you will."

19.

William DeKirk swallowed the last of a still-twitching meal, hungrily chewing it into digestible pieces and then ingesting them wholesale in several giant gulps. After wiping his lips on a piece of his last meal's shirt—a green golf polo—he sat back down in the great leather swivel chair. His hunger momentarily satisfied, he returned his attention to the screens, the giant monitors all split into multiple scenes, varied locations and news feeds.

It was all going so well.

Baltimore was a smoking ruin. It looked like a mob riot had spilled out from the stadium and now overran the city. So many people...zombies, he corrected himself. He sensed their need, the driving power behind the ancient force.

Atlanta was a war zone where a line of National Guard forces, including a pair of tanks, tried to hold off a countless mass of zombies, ragtag but powerfully fast, some cut down but then replaced just as quickly. There was air power—helicopters and a few F/A-18s, but they were unwilling to fire on the populated regions yet. Which was just as DeKirk expected. They were circling, trying to zero in their efforts on the dreadnought—which, as DeKirk hoped, was drawing their attention and leaving the infection free to spread even faster elsewhere.

The dreadnought, he was sure, could also hold its own. It was nimble, fast and so damn big that not much could bring it down. It was crunching through residential and commercial areas, preventing a full scale attack upon it for fear of harming civilians.

Sure, it wasn't born a carnivore, but the hunger and bloodlust had been instilled in it from the prions all the same, and its sheer destructiveness was more than sufficient for DeKirk's purposes.

He had the advantage. The pilots and the military would be too cautious. Unprepared and unwilling to do what had to be done. Waiting for commands that were too long in coming. The only way they could win, the only way to stop the spread of the infection, would be to firebomb the afflicted areas. Maybe even nuke selected cities.

No way. The president was a wild card, but even he wouldn't take such drastic action. At least not at first, and by the time his advisors warned him that there was no other option, it would be too late. The spread was inevitable, unstoppable.

Entirely unstoppable, DeKirk thought, smiling and licking his lips, still tasting the delicious iron-infused tang of his last meal.

He switched his gaze to Washington, where the battle was currently fiercest. Where *T. rexes* rampaged amidst cars and police on a congested street. Zombies climbed one of the beasts and leapt madly off its shoulders into the crowd of human defenders, and everywhere mayhem ruled. It was almost too much to take in, like watching multiple action movies simultaneously, but DeKirk's enhanced vision absorbed detail after detail.

It was good. So perfect, this army of his. Ruthless, relentless, indefatigable. Unstoppable.

Police, National Guard, and army units were set up at intersections, firing madly into the zombie mob or aiming for the faster moving crylos, but everywhere they were overrun—flanked by other dinosaurs, dive-bombed by pteros or assaulted from within, their own members changed, now one of the enemy after close battle.

On yet another screen, DeKirk called up a real-time satellite feed of Pennsylvania Avenue. He watched with grim satisfaction as the wave of zombies, following and riding along with a pair of *T. rexes,* strode up the street, oblivious to the defenses, to the armored cars and tanks and turrets that cut down hundreds of undead, but eventually fell prey to overwhelming numbers and relentless, unflagging brute force.

One *T. rex* was shredded through with heavy fire and missing huge hunks of flesh from its side, while the other was nothing more than a bullet sponge, its muscles and sinews shot to pulp, but they both seemed unfazed, still driven by primordial bloodlust and unquenchable hunger, and an ancient need to follow instinct.

Or, in this case, instructions. Biologically coded and enhanced neural instructions.

They had their target, answering the call from DeKirk's programming, and they in turn issued similar instructions but on a much simpler scale to all those even more mindless prion-infused hosts. The zombie humans that followed and swept along in their wake, headed toward a singular destination at the end of the avenue. With the glimmering white dome of the Capitol behind them, they headed toward the stark obelisk of the Washington Monument, rushing en masse toward...

The White House.

The defenses in that area would be the strongest, and already DeKirk saw the fleet of helicopters hovering ready, and knew there were more tanks and more teams of elite soldiers standing ready.

Ready to withstand most armies.

He smiled.

His was not most armies.

Directing his attention to another screen—captured video over the banks of the Potomac— he observed the fighting in the air. F/A-18s zipping across the sky, tangling with more agile pterodactyls that retained some base sense of self-preservation and evasiveness. Ducking and swooping, merging into forests and out and back, sweeping through the city even, leading the planes away from the open sky where their advantage was strongest.

Enough cat and mouse, DeKirk thought. Enough distraction for the planes.

His air power was needed elsewhere.

With the click of a few keys, he initiated a pulse to the neural chips embedded in the pteros' brain stems, activating a complex biological sequence of peptides and fast-release hormonal chemicals. Their senses were stimulated and augmented, and like migratory birds, their targeting system changed and a new destination beckoned intensely.

Fly, DeKirk thought. Time to neutralize the Capitol's air supremacy. After which the zombie horde, converging from all angles, led by the most vicious carnivores ever to walk the planet, would do the rest.

#

A few minutes, and he could watch it all unfold...

In the meantime, a check on that other metropolis he wanted to fall—and fall fast. It would be far easier to take New York, though not as satisfying at the end, but far more fun to watch.

Zombie-laden barges had burst through the blockades at four different points in Southern Jersey. Only a few crylos aboard, the bigger weapons not needed here, DeKirk had reasoned.

The congested city, the lack of defenses other than the valiant men and women of the NYPD and FDNY. They would be outmatched from the onset, and from what he could see of the various video feeds from CNN, local news and citizen video uploads, all splayed out on the next large screen, the Big Apple was rotting fast. Terror in the streets, mayhem in Times Square, Central Park in flames. People fleeing and trying to hold out in skyscrapers. That could happen, and certainly would be the last bastion of humanity…but they would soon be starved out and turn on each other or be fed upon by those outside.

DeKirk was more than patient, and when Washington had fallen and the final phase of his plan was firmly in place, he could mop up the remaining resistance at his leisure.

First, however, a blinking light on his secure line.

He pressed the button, wondering which of his lackeys was reporting in now.

"DeKirk! You have to get me! I'm on the U.N. rooftop, they've broken inside. You promised…"

"Hold your horses, Speaker Balsini." DeKirk rolled his eyes. Did he really promise this spineless cretin anything? And did it even matter?

Clicking a few keys, he accessed the U.N. cameras and bypassed their cyber-security measures through the passwords Balsini had supplied him with months earlier. There it was, the rooftop camera. He pulled up the video feed and saw Balsini, looking more than a little frazzled and worse for wear, way out of his element. Tie shredded, shirt bloodied.

"Looks like you had a little scuffle. Fight break out for the last donut at another catered lunch billed to the taxpayers?"

"You know damn well what's going on here! Thought you were going to give me a little more warning. I was in the middle of a briefing and…aggh." The Speaker doubled over, holding his gut. Then straightened up, shaking off the pain. The sun was intense up there, and DeKirk couldn't get a good look at Balsini's eyes.

"Uh… could you move a little to your left? Into the shade, Speaker. If you please?"

"What?" He shuffled a little to his left, out of the direct glare. "Just get me the goddamned chopper like you promised and fly me the hell out of here."

He winced again, then looked up and craned his neck, as if looking over the edge of the roof. "It's madness out there."

"Beautiful madness," DeKirk said, taking control of the camera, leaning forward some more, tapping a few keys.

"It happened so fast. Did you know it would be that fast? I mean, dear God, from the barge landing to those…things…overrunning half the city? What the hell, man! Are you sure you can handle this, that we can control…"

"Hang on, Speaker, you're moving too much. Stand still a second."

"What? Why?"

DeKirk adjusted the camera again, focusing and then zooming in on a section of the Speaker's shirt, just below the shoulder. A shredded piece of silk, and…

"There it is."

"There what is?" Balsini jerked backwards, grunted and coughed up blood, a viscous flow down his chin. "Ugh, what the—?"

"I'm sorry, Mr. Speaker but I'm going to reroute that chopper."

Balsini looked up, eyes in pain, reddening with flecks of yellow, but holding on to some flash of hope. He scanned the sky. "To get it here faster?"

"Sorry, but no. I thank you for your service so far, Mr. Speaker, and I thank you for your service to come. Which will be in a different, much more mindless fashion."

"What the hell do you mean? What…"

He choked, fell to his knees and tried to look down at himself, at his torn shirt.

"You're looking a bit pale, my friend. Take a load off, have a seat. Won't be long now."

Balsini did as he was told. Sat with a groan, pulled his knees up to his bloody chin, and started to rock as he gazed up, without blinking now, his eyes reflecting the color of the sun.

"Will it take long?"

DeKirk licked his lips. "As you said before, and noticed so keenly, this happens *fast*. Just sit tight, you'll be a new man soon enough."

DeKirk clicked a button to minimize the screen while he returned his attention to the larger focus at Washington. He'd keep the U.N. rooftop view up just to witness the Speaker's change, because no matter how many times he'd seen it before, it was still a fascinating transformation, like a caterpillar to butterfly in super speed, and every bit as symbolically perfect.

He flexed his fingers, tightened his jaw muscles and stretched his sinewy arms, still philosophizing on the comparison.

The slow and useless worm transformed into a creature of limitless power and potential.

And beauty.

20.

In the air over Washington, D.C.

Major Remington descended in formation—or what was left of his formation. Starting with six jets in the air, they were down to three. Two crashed into the Atlantic and the third slammed into one of those damned pterodactyls in mid-air, taking out both.

"Three bogies ahead!" Remington shouted, locking the targeting on one. Strafing the bird's head with machine gun fire worked well, but so would a heat-seeking Sidewinder down its throat. Blow off its arm-like wings and it would still live, but it was going nowhere, biting no one and dropping no more payloads.

These *things...* He shook his head and regained his composure as his colleagues opened fire on the targets.

Damn, they were nimble. The winged reptiles arcing out of the way just in time, their hides taking some damage but not much as they rolled, ducked and split directions effortlessly. It was like trying to swat a fly in mid-air; they knew where the attack was coming from and expertly tilted just far enough out of the way.

"AIM-9s!" Remington called to the other pilots. "Take 'em down with heat-seekers!"

If we can lock on long enough, that is. His target lock was lost already, before he could fire. He zipped over a smoking section of Fairfax and passed within visual of Reagan International Airport—where he heard all planes had been rerouted to the country's interior, to places like Iowa or Mississippi. The streets all along the way, and wherever he could see, seemed peaceful from this level, but as soon as he dipped lower, chaos ruled.

Roads congested and bottlenecked, cars abandoned and blocking any further traffic. Some bodies lying about on the streets or lawns, but mostly...those killed had gotten back up, enlisted in the service of the opposition, minds no longer their own. Great hordes swelled into even ranks and marched with purpose, zone by zone, looking like a colony of ants from this height. Ants with a collective hive mind, serving a central authority figure, branching this way and that, racing through neighborhoods, breaking through windows, rooting out panicked and screaming residents.

Everything here was compromised, and Remington wondered how long it could be until he received an order to start firing upon the city itself? Or would they just call their forces back and send in the bigger guns from carriers at sea, or from NORAD itself?

He banked around again and ascended, mercifully giving his eyes a break and a clear view of the peaceful sky above, but only for a moment and then it was over, back to scanning for targets.

"Where the hell are they?"

"Broke formation and fled," radioed one of his colleagues in the air. "Looks like they're weaving around and going low, dive-bombing?"

"No more payloads," said the third pilot. "I've got a visual and I'm in pursuit. Looks like they're heading toward Pennsylvania Avenue."

"Shit," Remington spat. "Take them out, first chance! I'm right behind you, and—*look out!*"

"Wha-?" The pilot couldn't get another syllable out as a black streaking shape hurtled up from a copse of trees. A ptero that had been perched there, preparing to spring. It crunched hard into the left wing, its beak tilted so it rammed the fighter at an upward angle.

The F/A-18's wing shattered and the entire fuselage erupted in flames and smoke. Its nose tilted and it went down—veering left, then nose-diving into a ball of fire and wreckage.

"No!" Remington and the last pilot shouted together. Fumbling for control, he tried to lock on to the ptero that had done the damage. Its wing was on fire—another good source of heat for the missile's tracking.

"I'm locked on," said the other pilot, who fired immediately, diving from above, and then swooping up. The injured bird hugged its wings to its body and dropped, diving toward a populated section of Pennsylvania avenue... swooping for a convoy of tanks setting up a line of defense.

Oh no, Remington thought.

The dinosaur opened its wings—one of them still smoldering—at the last second, flattened out, then rammed the lead tank, knocking it sideways.

That in itself wouldn't have done anything, except the heat-seeking missile right on its tail impacted a moment later, erupting into an enormous fireball of carnage that took out the tank and three of its neighbors, raining searing hot wreckage on a full contingent of soldiers.

Cursing, Remington peeled out, seeking the other three pteros, but before he could locate them something in the river caught his eye. A Coast Guard vessel, valiantly bombarding the shore and a pair of crylos wreaking havoc there, was suddenly upended and capsized.

The shark-thing, Remington saw, and his fury mounted. The word *mesosaur*, one he'd heard in an all-too-quick briefing, flashed through his brain. Did he have time? He could surely bomb that thing and take it out, freeing up the harbor for safe entrance by reinforcements, but his orders were to protect the White House.

He zipped ahead, swerved down low, around the Washington Monument, and prepared to make another run down Pennsylvania Avenue, over the remaining fighters and resistance. He would provide air bombardment and weaken the onrushing hordes, using every missile and round at his disposal.

He checked the radar for other aircraft—F/A-18s or enemy fliers. There was Nielson, in the jet, locked in a dogfight with one of the pteros. Six Apache helicopters also entered the fray, coming in fast from the south, bringing a smile to Remington's lips.

Good, might have time now for a little fishing...

One pass down the avenue, unleash a few missiles, and then he'd bank for the river—

A jarring impact.

NO!

Another one of those damn birds, rising from below, this time behind the cover of a building. It just clipped a tail fin, but it was enough to throw off his balance and send the altimeter spinning. He wasn't going to make it. Couldn't rise, couldn't turn.

Son of a—

He could at least steer and aim down.

There…

A *T.rex* leading the charge.

Remington armed his missiles, all of them. Accelerated—then hit the eject button.

He never saw the impact, never got to witness what he could only have imagined was quite a stellar display of destruction of U.S. government property, an F/A-18 Super Hornet colliding with a *T.rex*, exploding with about 1,000 gallons of jet fuel and four armed AIM-9 missiles.

The detonation, however, lifted his seat and the blast caught his parachute, launching him backwards hundreds of yards…

… out of immediate danger, over the army's perimeter defenses, and into the encampment fronting the White House.

He tumbled, rolling hard and painfully on his shoulders and knees but then got to his feet, running and stumbling until someone caught him and other soldiers put out the fire on his parachute.

"Nice one," someone said, and at last he looked up and back— to the huge cloud of fiery intensity and the skeletal thing that stumbled out of it, then literally fell apart, incinerated to dust.

"Took out a damn tyrannosaurus," another soldier said.

Remington coughed and shook his head, then pointed. "There's another one. Pterodactyls, too. Patch me through to those Apaches before they're surprised and taken out."

Someone raced to comply, getting a transmitter, when Remington heard the first of the choppers.

Relief, however, turned sour fast as two of the war machines went down, attacked from flanking positions by a squadron of pteros almost as soon as they were within range.

"Goddamnit! Get me…"

More screams sounded behind him, more gunfire, and out of the smoke and fire roared the other *T.rex*, and the rest of the zombie horde.

21.

Alex's mind had trouble processing how quickly and how thoroughly things had deteriorated since he was last outside. He and Veronica stood on the steps outside the CIA building watching a kaleidoscope of strife and civil mayhem. The scale of chaos was like nothing they had ever seen. Where their struggles on Adranos had been set in largely a rainforest environment against isolated contingents of zombies and a few rogue dinosaurs, here they were suddenly in the midst of a concrete jungle in seemingly endless urban disarray.

Somewhere beneath the street, a gas main had ruptured and tongues of flame shot up from the subterranean level through an open manhole cover. Downed power lines were everywhere, many sparking blue arcs of electricity where they fell. The road itself was utter bedlam with vehicles disabled and toppled on their sides making it impassable to normal traffic. There were people about, too, only in most cases, Alex saw, they weren't really people anymore. Zombies reigned, far more numerous than the living. Worse, they seemed to be capable of more organization than the undead he'd witnessed on Adranos.

There were no more one-on-one attacks; the zombies had somehow learned to assault in coordinated fashion like pack animals—probably like some of the dinosaur species that also rioted through the streets, through an environment for which they were never intended but now roamed as if in complete control. Two zombies would converge on a victim from either side, rather than both of them plodding mindlessly at the human. The behavior was definitely new.

Alex looked at Veronica, who stood by his side, equally stunned as she took in the rampant devastation. "How far is that airfield?"

"Two-and-a-half miles." Her mouth tugged downward at the corners as she contemplated the significance of that distance through this carnage.

"What choice do we have?"

Alex continued to survey the damage. He was wary of a group of four zombies who had eviscerated an African-American woman wearing a parking cop uniform. Her little scooter car lay turned on its side nearby, ticket book pages loose everywhere, some stuck in place on the pavement by her own coagulating blood, and one—the last ticket she ever wrote—still affixed beneath the windshield wiper of a parked SUV, a citation representing a government now in its death throes.

The undead fought in sporadic mini-bouts over what was left of the meter maid. Their heads were looking around more now, no longer riveted to the gory meal. Alex froze with a jolt of adrenaline as one of them, wearing a stained and tattered three-piece suit, actually made yellow-tinged eye contact with him.

"Veronica?"

"Yeah."

"We've got to move."

Wordlessly she slipped off the steps to their left, signaling for him to follow. He crept after her, unable to resist glancing back at the suited zombie. It was a mistake, for the additional eye contact incensed the creature, who stood with a grunt and actually lifted an arm in Alex and Veronica's direction. Alex turned around in time to see two zombies step out from behind a rental box truck missing a front wheel. One of them had an umbrella sticking out of its thigh and walked with a severe limp a few steps behind the other, which gave Alex a pang of sadness upon seeing a young woman who must have been of high school age wearing a man's leather jacket.

Then he heard the staccato *rat-tat-tat* from Veronica's AK-47 and the former cheerleader was cut down in a hail of lead, parts of her face speckling the yellow siding of the truck. Veronica ejected one magazine and replaced it with another she'd picked off a fallen SWAT guy. Alex focused on locating the suit zombie within the sights of his pistol. It took him four shots, but he ended up dropping the oncoming threat with a bullet to the forehead.

"C'mon. Main highway's over there. Look for a working vehicle with keys."

Most of the cars and trucks were overturned or had obvious defects. A few, though, were simply parked and locked, such as the SUV with the ticket. He could probably smash a window and try to hotwire one, but meanwhile more zombies were pouring into the area. It would be a real battle with no guarantees.

They made their way down the street and turned onto a larger one. In the intersection, a small platoon of National Guardsman was set up as a mobile command center. They had a large militarized RV-type vehicle, armored and with serious firepower as well as an array of antennae on the roof. Parked around it were a few Humvees and a large square tent, open with men inside gesturing as they yelled into phones and stared wide-eyed at screens.

And with good reason. There weren't quite as many zombies here as the street with the CIA building, but two crylopholosaurs were holding court around the intersection, stamping on cars, rushing at people, braying into the night.

"I'm so sick of those damn things," Alex commented to Veronica.

In response, she pointed silently at a Humvee with no doors or windows and a machine gun mounted in back that was just rolling up to the RV. Four soldiers occupied the seats with a fifth manning the gun, firing off controlled bursts into the dinosaurs. They watched as the driver put it in park but left the engine running. He and the other four soldiers jumped from the vehicle and made for the RV, firing off rounds at zombies from handguns and automatic rifles as they went.

Alex tapped Veronica on the shoulder and nodded toward the Humvee. *Our ride?* Her eyes widened in response. Normally, it would be inconceivable to steal an armed military vehicle in the midst of a manned field station, but they had left Normal far, far behind. She glanced around the area, especially at the tent and at the RV, before nodding.

"You drive, I'll handle the gun."

Alex nodded his approval and she went on hurriedly. "Head down that street there..." She pointed past a building on fire and a toppled street light. "...and then take the next left."

Alex studied the route for a couple of seconds and gave a resolute nod. "On three...two...run quiet!...one, go!"

The pair dashed toward the Humvee. They reached it without incident and Veronica jumped into the back with the mounted gun while Alex took his seat behind the wheel. As soon as he sat down, the two-way radio in the vehicle blared with some technical chatter, causing him to jump in alarm.

"Go!" Veronica urged.

He put the Humvee into gear and rolled quietly at low speed out onto an unobstructed portion of the street. Alex was about to floor it when he saw an old man desperately trying to fight off three zombies with a cane in one hand and a pocketknife in the other. The man turned in circles with shaky, uncertain movements while the undead attackers outpaced him in all directions. Alex pulled up to the fracas.

"What are you doing?" Veronica swiveled the gun around on the back of the hummer, looking for signs of serious trouble.

"Helping this guy out. *Hey c'mon*, jump in!"

The old man dodged between the circle of zombies with speed that belied his age, probably triggered by the sight of help arrived. He flung himself into the passenger seat and muttered words of thanks as Alex got back on the road.

"Alex, what if he's been bitten?"

"We're going to drop him off at the next safe-looking place we see." Then, to their new passenger, "Hey, you okay?"

He felt along the sleeves of his shirt while he answered. "Not bitten. Not really okay, either. I always said I dreaded the boredom they say comes with old age, but I'd take a long night in the nursing home any day compared to this nightmare. You in the Army?" He gave Alex and Veronica's dirty and blood-splattered civilian clothes a doubting stare.

Alex cracked a smile as he responded while gunning the engine. "Don't ask don't tell,' pal, okay?" He made the left Veronica told him about and saw a relatively calm stretch ahead. He pulled over and looked at the man.

"This is where you get off. Zombie Free Zone, at least for now."

"Where are you guys heading?" The old man didn't try to disguise his reluctance about leaving the safety of the vehicle.

"That's classified, sir," Alex said with all the seriousness he could muster. "But believe me when I say you wouldn't have a good time where we're going."

"I suppose not," the man said, stepping out of the truck.

"Get inside somewhere and wait this out," Veronica advised.

"One last favor?" the man called up to her. He looked around, forlorn and lost.

"What?"

"Shoot me with that big gun of yours."

At length, Alex replied, "Just go inside, sir, you'll be all right." But inwardly he wondered how true that statement really was. Veronica swung the hardware away from the man, toward the intersection they'd just turned through.

"Seriously. I've had a good life, until recently. Everyone I knew was already dead before any of this happened. Only reason I'm outside is because a bunch of those crazies got inside the home and tore it to pieces. If things don't get back to normal, well then, you saw back there what's going to happen to me. You saved me this time, but next time I'll be on my own. I'd much rather you just cut my damn head off with that big gun of yours than go through what I was about to with those ghoulish things."

He walked around to the opening of the gun barrel. "I'm joking, but really I'm not."

"Alex!"

Looking away from their sad previous passenger, Alex recognized the tone in Veronica's voice, that tone that said, regardless of the words it carried, *bad shit is about to go down right now.*

Alex had been looking ahead through the windshield, where all was clear. Looked nice and drivable, only a couple of upended vehicles that could easily be maneuvered around. He twisted around in the driver's seat and looked out the back, where the old man was still looking around, despondent and suicidal.

But that wasn't what held his attention.

Around the intersection, they could see the head of a *T. rex.* Just the head, sticking over the corner of a two-story building, looking down on them on this street while the bulk of its body and its feet were still on the other street. It had the same rotten-looking hide as the one they'd barely escaped from on the runway at Adranos, and even from this distance the yellow tint to its eyes was clearly distinct.

"I see it. Time to go." Alex turned around to put the Hummer into gear.

"Alex! It's moving!"

He didn't need her to tell him because he could hear the gigantic lizard's feet slapping the pavement as it hopped around the corner to the street they were on.

"Help!" the old man cried out as he dropped to his knees before the rampaging beast's approach. "Now!" He broke down into uncontrollable sobs, his face in the pavement.

The *T. rex* saw the Hummer start to roll and jumped toward it, head low to the ground. The old man glanced back as he heard the Hummer accelerate away, then swung around to look at the dinosaur.

Veronica aimed the heavy gun at the tyrannosaur, unleashing a frightening bullet hose of fire the likes of which she had no experience in controlling, rounds that punched into the reanimated animal's muscular chest while a few bullets went stray and wide into upper level edifices on their right side. The terrible lizard halted its forward progress mere feet behind the old man, who was now crying softly while covering his face.

The *T. rex* made a sharp hissing noise that reminded Alex of an air brake on a bus. He glanced at the creature in the rear view mirror as Veronica tore into it with a fresh volley from the mounted 50-cal. The shots were finding their mark, pummeling the massive reptile in the head, beginning to open the skull up entirely, when Alex drove through a large pothole that had escaped his notice while he looked into the mirror.

The resulting motion had the effect on Veronica's gun of jerking it first up—where the rounds skewed skyward—and then sharply back down, stitching along the reptile's body and lower still, where they found the head and body of the old man. He did an involuntary, violent dance from his kneeling position on the street while the projectiles ripped away the back of his skull.

Then the *T. rex* stumbled—tripped, really—and toppled, landing on the old man and crushing out of him whatever vestiges of life remained.

"Oh God," Veronica said simply, knowing the old man could no longer hear her, and knowing that he had gotten what he had asked for, but it wasn't her choice to make. "I'm sorry."

She would have enough wrenching decisions to make going forward without making them by accident for other people.

22.

Alex said nothing, his eyes darting to the mirror and back to the road. He drove the Hummer the rest of the way to the air base in stunned silence without major incident. Veronica only fired the gun a couple of times the rest of the way.

Once there, though, it became apparent that accessing the facility would be anything but easy. A veritable war zone greeted them, but not any normal theater of war. Here, men waged battle against near mythical beasts. Pterodactyls wheeled in the air above the facility while crylos rampaged across the ground, intermingling with human zombies who attempted to breach the facility gate. A few of the crylos had zombie riders atop their backs, their dull eyes fixed ahead as their slacked and rotting jaws drooled syrupy fluid. A full contingent of soldiers fought against this hybrid army from a fleet of vehicles as well as a guard post at the entrance to the compound. Beyond this gate a paved road continued about a quarter-mile until it branched out into an assortment of low-lying buildings.

Veronica stepped away from the gun and held up her CIA badge high. She saw a loudspeaker mounted on the front of the truck and asked Alex to use it. He picked up the radio transmitter, handed it back to Veronica, and flipped on the PA switch.

"This is CIA Special Agent Veronica Winters. I have been ordered to report here to board a plane along with my associate. Our orders are to fly to Atlanta."

The reply came in the form of a clipped male voice over a PA system of their own. "Agent Winters: glad you made it. Proceed at once *with extreme caution* to the main guard post."

Alex wasted no time speeding off in the Hummer before a group of coordinated zombies could reach their vehicle. Veronica blasted out intense bursts from the 50-cal into groups of undead as well as a dive-bombing ptero that came too low for comfort. Bullets shredded one of its wings and the bird-like reptile fell into the ground, unable to glide, where it collided with a crylo that promptly and inadvertently stamped the ptero's skull open.

Under cover fire, Alex skidded to a stop in front of the gate, clouds of dust billowing up from the Humvee's wheels. Veronica blasted one more group of oncoming zombies with the mounted gun, and then she and Alex ran the few steps to the guard house, where a tall soldier in combat fatigues held out a hand to Veronica—not to shake her hand but to inspect her credentials. She extended the card on the lanyard but did not remove it from her neck. The soldier eyeballed the picture and his eyes bounced from the card to her face and back.

"Agent Winters, the plane is waiting for you inside the gate on the airstrip. Hop in the Jeep, I'll take you—short ride to the end of the field over there."

Alex and Veronica looked to where the soldier pointed and were dismayed to see a battle playing out there as well. A small airplane sat on a paved airstrip with a battalion of soldiers fighting a *T. rex* (the one already riddled with 50 cal bullets) as well as a horde of remotely controlled zombies. They were keeping the enemy at bay for now but to Alex it didn't look like they could hold out for much longer before the plane would be damaged or completely destroyed. The pilot-side door was open too, Alex noted.

Veronica grabbed him by the hand, urging him to get in the Jeep.

"He's with you?" the soldier asked, giving Alex a cautious look.

"Yeah, is that a problem?"

He finished his appraisal and shook his head. "You're cleared for two passengers besides yourself." With that, Alex and Veronica hopped into the back of the open vehicle. The soldier got behind the wheel while his associate in the guard post pressed a switch that started the entrance gate closing. Alex asked how the zombies had already gotten past the gate.

The soldier turned his head sideways from his position behind the wheel while they bounced along toward the waiting plane. "The pterodactyls dropped the humanoids inside, and the *T. rex*...well, we've learned a *T. rex* pretty much goes where it wants to go."

As Alex took in the crushed perimeter fence, topped with razor wire that now lay on the ground, he knew exactly what the military man was saying. Urgent-sounding, jargon-laced chatter burst from the Jeep's radio as they braked to a stop in front of the plane. Alex recognized it as a Beechcraft Baron, a four-seat twin turboprop with a decent range.

"This thing fueled for the trip?" Alex asked.

"You bet. Topped off and ready to go. Mechanic gave her the blessing just a couple of hours ago. That plane is probably the only thing you *don't* need to worry about." He pointed to the aircraft, making it clear that he would not be getting out of the Jeep. "Get going and good luck!"

Alex eyed the towering *T. rex* that stood maybe two hundred feet from the plane, surrounded by a contingent of soldiers peppering it with automatic weapons fire that seemed to have little effect. Alex watched as one of the men shouldered a rocket launcher and aimed it at the beast.

"Where's the pilot?" Alex eyed the empty cockpit, wondering if he'd be called upon once more to show off his flying skills.

The soldier pointed off to their left, where a man in an aviator's jumpsuit backpedaled as he fired a pistol at a pursuing zombie group. "He's ready, don't worry. Just board the aircraft."

Alex and Veronica took off running to the plane, Veronica squeezing off a couple of rounds at a pterodactyl that had crash-landed on the ground between them and the plane and snapped at them on broken bones as they sidled past.

They reached the plane and Alex opened the rear door and helped Veronica up inside, then got in after her. He glanced over at the *T. rex,* which now looked like it was about to collapse at any moment under continued assault of heavy arms fire. Then the pilot came running up to the plane, still firing his pistol.

A middle-aged man sporting a buzz cut and mirrored aviator's sunglasses, the pilot jumped behind the wheel and yanked the door shut. His hands flew over the controls while he spoke to his two passengers without turning around.

"Name's Atkinson, call me Skip. Buckle up, next stop Atlanta." That was the extent of his introduction. He continued throwing switches and pressing buttons in preparation for takeoff as the whine of the engines increased in pitch. As he reached up to press a button on the ceiling console, Alex tapped Veronica's leg and nodded his head toward the pilot's bare arm.

A nasty-looking chunk of flesh was missing just below the elbow, the surrounding skin smeared with blood. Before Veronica could react, the pilot's hands were on the wheel and the plane was turning slowly as it taxied into takeoff position on the runway.

Veronica pointed. "Pterodactyl, incoming! It's diving on us!"

The pilot gunned the engine and the plane hurtled down the airstrip, rapidly gaining speed and momentum. The passengers bounced in their seats as the aircraft approached takeoff velocity while the radio erupted with base chatter.

Veronica took Alex's hand and squeezed it as a ptero dashed across the plane's forward path, missing the nose by scant feet. The pilot picked up the radio transmitter and shouted into it that he was taking off. Veronica turned to Alex, nodding at the pilot's arm wound.

In a muffled voice in his ear, she asked: "Can you fly one of these?"

23.

Washington, D.C.

From his position inside the M1A1 tank, Major Casey Remington surveyed the devastation on Pennsylvania Avenue on a monitor displaying a live video feed of what transpired outside. He'd never seen anything like it, that was for sure. A full-on war zone raged on U.S. soil—in the U.S. capital city, no less. *Unbelievable.*

Yet his monitor didn't lie. The pain-addled screams of his soldiers didn't lie. The firefight raging outside the White House fence didn't lie. Most of all, the hellish menagerie of prehistoric animals with their cohort of zombie-like humanoids Did Not Lie.

For just a moment he thought of his daughter, of Olivia who hadn't even been named a few short days ago. He thought of his wife, thought of the millions of Americans glued together with the common emotion of fear. Not since 9/11 had so many the world over been focused on the same thing, but he knew this was it, this was different. This was potentially the End of Everything.

He didn't know what he, just one fighter, could do, but he had to try. He ordered the tank gunner to launch another mortar at the *T. rex* loose on the avenue. The 120mm smoothbore projectile impacted on its shoulders, exploding and severing the head so badly that it flopped loose against the body although the creature continued to walk about. "Again!" he rallied his gunner. The second shot hit the rib cage and detonated, blasting the head off completely; it dropped from the body to the street where it lay with its yellow eyes open, gnashing its ridiculously long teeth at a passing military truck.

An entire convoy of armored vehicles currently blasted away at an army of zombies all intent on breaching the White House fence. They didn't have the ability to free climb it, but once enough of them had been killed so that the bodies were piling up, the still living zombies were able to use the corpses as a crude step ladder. One zombie managed to jump from the top of the pile to reach the fence's top crossbar, one of the spikes passing through its wrist. From there, it pulled itself up while the shooters riddled its body with lead.

"Tell those guys to go for the head! The head!" Remington snarled into his radio from inside the tank.

The adjustment was made, but not before that particular zombie earned the distinction of being the first of the undead to land on the White House lawn before its cranium was shattered by a Marine's armor-piercing round and it dropped dead, once and for all, on one of the most heavily guarded properties on the planet.

It would not be the last.

Remington ordered the tank to start rolling again. It made him nervous to remain stationary for more than a few minutes. He scanned the digital data map and tried to analyze all the intel and the rush of data scrolling on his screen. Orders and counter-orders, a confusing, rapidly changing list of priorities. The sheer speed with which everything had gone so wrong had been dizzying. A series of staccato beeps was heard in the tank and the communications operator tapped Remington on the shoulder.

"Delta Team reporting in that Bravo has fallen back. They couldn't hold the Washington Monument, sir. They were overrun, numerous casualties and many of them are now…" The operator hesitated, apparently seeking the right words.

"Are now *what*, soldier?" Remington regretted asking as soon as he did. He knew, and shouldn't have made the poor soldier speak it aloud, but maybe the truth would harden his resolve.

"Are now part of the opposition, sir." He took a breath, then regained his composure, and gave an update that Remington hadn't heard before. "Prelim reports indicate that the newly infected dead don't have the coordination abilities of those in the initial waves. Medical teams report that some of the dissected field specimens indicate circuitry components that the newly dead won't have, but they're still…zombies, for lack of a better word, sir, that spread the contagion."

Circuitry. Jesus, then this is all directed, a massive terrorist attack of pure calculated evil. Remington fought off a wave of nausea. Every time he thought he was making an inch of progress, he found out that they had just lost a mile. He tapped a monitor that currently displayed diagnostic information about the tank.

"Do we have drones in the sky?"

The operator nodded.

"Patch me in the video feed from it, can you?"

"Will do, sir." He set about completing the task while Remington turned and peered into the viewer, adjusting its optics for a direct view of the tank's immediate surroundings. It had infrared sensors for night time, but he certainly didn't need that option now. Zombies were everywhere, including, he noticed with a taste of bile in his throat, some of whom only minutes earlier had been his own fellow marines.

He heard a screech and turned his attention to the sky, where a pterodactyl zoomed in low over the White House fence with a zombie rider on its back. One of the tank's gunners took a strafing run at it but missed, and the ptero deposited its undead payload deep onto the White House property from a few feet above ground.

"Major, sir! I've got that drone feed up now."

Remington shifted his attention to the monitor that showed an aerial view of the greater D.C. environs, and felt his breath catch.

It was unfathomable, the number of undead and dinosaurs, and the organization with which they moved—*marched*—on the capital. This wasn't a mere army, it was an invasion force from another world. Reminiscent of medieval warfare tactics, a boxy phalanx of perhaps a thousand zombie soldiers, flanked on all sides and in the air by a squadron of reanimated dinosaurs, made its way toward the Capitol Building.

One of his officers alerted him to the monitor that visualized the environment just outside the tank. "Sir, more pterodactyls, incoming!"

Remington broke away from the scope. "Where are the remaining Apaches?" He had seen from the support logs that additional air support had been ordered thirty minutes earlier.

"On the way, sir. I see one of them on the way now."

"One? Where are the others?"

"Diverted to the main force at the Monument, sir, or…lost in battle already."

Remington eyeballed the live feed again. Before today, he didn't think it was possible for any living thing to give an Apache trouble, but as he watched two pteros launch themselves—apparently with deliberation—into the main rotor assembly of the helicopter, he changed his mind. The chopper exploded over the White House itself, raining flaming debris onto the roof of the presidential residence.

"Goddamn it!"

The two surviving pteros flew across the White House lawn, over the fence and out over the tank, where strafing fire shot one of them down. It landed in a crumpled heap of shattered bones and torn membranes on the street. The other ptero managed to avoid fire and hit the ground running, where two zombies jumped atop its back. Then it took off again, turning back over the fence toward the White House. When it neared the porch of the historic building, it came in low and its riders dropped off onto the ground, where they fanned out in opposite directions around the house.

The ptero was cut down on the ground by automatic weapons fire from the White House roof. The reprieve didn't last long, however, for alarmed shouts soon warned Remington of a new aerial attack.

"More pterodactyls, inbound—high and fast!"

"Mortars, strafing runs, fire at will. Hit 'em with everything we got!" Remington balled his hands into tight fists while he consulted a radar screen depicting the six new targets approaching the White House. Then, on the video feed, he watched as an object fell from one of the pteros. It was small, but it gave Remington a big chill.

"Take cover! Possible bombardment."

Outside, a scuba-tank-sized canister fell from one of the pteros into a military staging area on Pennsylvania Avenue. The object exploded and soldiers nearby were cut down, hit by shrapnel.

"Bomb!" came the report over the radio from the staging area commander.

Remington watched in disbelief as five more of the bombs were dropped by the other winged reptiles. "More incoming!" he shouted in reply.

The pteros were all shot down but it was too late. Their deadly payloads dropped and multiple explosions rocked the famous street, releasing a storm of metal fragments into the soldiers and emergency personnel who fronted the White House.

"Multiple friendlies down, casualties confirmed," came the initial report.

But that was not the worst of it.

Minutes later, while still reeling from the attack and while Remington and his tank crew were busy pounding at distant targets and softening up the army of approaching zombies, the first of the dead soldiers rose from the ground.

Remington again had to doubt his senses. "These marines...they weren't bitten. They've only been dead for a few minutes, How is this possible?"

The operator beside him took a look. "Sir...I don't know! I've had them in visual the whole time."

"Those frag bombs..." said the radar tech, "they must have been already infected with the contagion."

The words hung there with all of the smoke in the air above the tank. The notion was uncomfortable as hell.

"Biological warfare," Remington muttered. Before he could say anything else, a new scene of bloody carnage unfolded on the live feed. The newly dead soldiers began biting those charged with tending to the dead and wounded, turning on their own so fast the medics couldn't even react. By the time the others realized it and began fighting back, it was too late. It only took a single bite to spread the prion infection. Soon, many more soldiers were dead men walking, right in the midst of the defenders who now had to contend with the external attack as well as internal. The newly initiated zombies were not under remote control influence, but were deadly free-ranging disease agents all the same.

A new directive came over the radio, addressed specifically to Major Remington: *get to the Capitol Building and defend it before it falls.*

With great regret, Remington took a last look at the soldiers taking messy chunks of meat from their associates—mindless, primal, beyond animalistic—and gave the orders to his men to move the tank out.

24.

Airborne en route to Atlanta, Georgia

Somewhere over Virginia, the pilot began to shows signs that he was undergoing the transformation. Oddly, the first clue was a slight change in the pitch of his voice. It became higher, more nasally, perhaps due to the constricting of his throat and arteries. Alex noticed it when the airman was calling out over the radio trying without success to reach a still-functioning air traffic control tower. Then his movements became noticeably sloth-like, more labored. He was slower to reach his arm out to adjust controls. His arm wound had worsened, too, developing a disturbing yellowish bruising pattern that oozed a clear goopy substance.

Definitely took longer to change after a bite than it did after death from a bite. If the host was still alive, apparently the immune resistance gave the victim some time at least, before succumbing.

Alex pointed the captain's change out to Veronica, who leaned over and whispered into his ear. "You got this, right?"

"I can fly it, just not that sure I can stick the landing. But this guy's not going to last much longer, so we either force him to land now or we take him out and hope I can figure out how to land later."

Veronica thought about this while her right hand crept along her thigh to the snap catch on her knife sheath. "If we land now, we'd have to figure out a new way to get all the way to Atlanta."

Alex had no counter to that. He had no idea how the rest of the East Coast (or hell, the entire country, for that matter) fared, but he certainly didn't relish the thought of travelling hundreds of miles through conditions like those they'd experienced for only a few of those miles.

With the barest whisper of steel sliding against leather, Veronica removed the KA-BAR fixed blade knife from its sheath.

Alex eyed the familiar-looking blade. "You still have that thing?"

"Souvenir from our island vacation," she said, flashing on a mental highlight reel of violent attacks that she quickly suppressed. It was time for a new assault. She shot Alex a look that said, *Be ready*.

The pilot began jerking his head up and down in a strange series of rapid movements. His radio erupted with a reply from the ground. As he reached for the transmitter, missing it and randomly swiping at a cluster of switches, Veronica sprung. She placed her blade where she knew it had to go in order to be effective—upward through the neck, inside the jawbone and directly into the brain cavity. Instantly, the brand new zombie had the life snuffed out of it. It slumped in the seat, blood dumping from its gaping neck and head wound as Veronica withdrew her knife. She wiped it quickly on the seat and returned it to its sheath.

The plane started to veer sharply to one side as the dead zombie slumped onto the steering column.

"Alex!"

He reached forward and tossed the former pilot into the passenger seat, and then he climbed over into the cockpit, taking the dead man's spot. He gripped the controls and leveled out the aircraft. "Can we eject this guy?" he called back to Veronica. "Don't really need a dead zombie co-pilot." She also moved up front.

"Put your belt on first," Alex cautioned. She did so and then she propped the corpse against the passenger-side door while Alex concentrated on flying the plane and familiarizing himself as best he could with the controls.

"Where's the latch on this thing?" Alex explained to her how it works and then told her he was holding the plane steady, ready when she was. Veronica hauled the body atop her lap and gripped the door latch with one hand.

"What are we flying over? Don't want to hit anybody with a dead zombie."

"Just a bunch of farmland. As good as it's going to get. You might hit a horse or something."

"Yippie ki-yay."

With a grunt, Veronica shoved the door open with an elbow and hauled the body across her lap. She gave it a good shove and sent it out, a skydiving zombie corpse. Veronica heaved the door shut and fell back into her seat, winded from the effort.

Alex looked down from his door window and spotted the undead cadaver-bomb, now a mere speck in the sky. Then he checked his compass heading and saw that he had gotten off course, and corrected for it.

"Back on track for Atlanta."

"So what about landing this thing when we get there?"

"Thanks, I was trying not to think about it."

"Is this really all that different from the planes—Cessnas and Sandpipers, right—that you know how to fly?"

Alex surveyed the instrument panel with a frown. "Afraid so."

Then the radio crackled with staticky voices. Veronica held her ear closer to the speaker, straining to hear the intermittent transmission.

"Sounds like other pilots asking which airports are still open with services…where are we now, do you know?" She looked out the window with a furrowed brow.

"North Carolina. We'll be in Georgia soon, and then Atlanta won't be far."

Veronica continued to scan the radio channels while Alex flew. They heard a few snatches of conversation here and there, but all in all, Alex remarked, the air bands were uncharacteristically silent. The next hour went in relative silence, neither of them speaking, knowing it still wasn't the time, and nothing else—dwelling on what had happened or speculating on things they couldn't verify—mattered. Veronica continued to tune in the frequencies, however, and as they crossed over the Georgia state line she got one to come in clear that featured a robotic, male voice.

"…residents and visitors advised to seek shelter immediately. The following cities have been designated as Temporary Shelter Zones: Chattanooga, Greenville, Athens, Dothan…"

The emergency bulletin droned on with a long list of smaller, inland cities.

"I don't hear Atlanta on the list." Veronica turned the volume down as the message began to repeat.

"Probably means that the major cities have been lost and the military and National Guard are now trying to save the second tier cities."

"Great."

Alex glanced out the windshield at the ground below, where structures became more numerous as they approached the greater Atlanta area.

"It's okay. We just have to get down there, near the CDC Headquarters building, and then we need to find this doctor...?"

"Arcadia Grey. Get her, along with her research materials. Hopefully she'll have herself and everything ready for extraction."

"And hopefully I can land this thing."

Suddenly Veronica heard something of interest and turned the radio back up.

"...underground NORAD facility near Cheyenne, Wyoming, one of the possible locations for a new seat of government, along with Cabinet members, the Joint Chiefs of Staff and leading science and technology experts. Once again, the White House has fallen, the president's condition is unknown, but the core operating government, we have been assured, including successor arrangements, are secure in a highly defensible underground bunker, possibly at a Wyoming NORAD facility, or perhaps at Raven Rock, Pennsylvania. There are many rumors flying around right now, but unfortunately, no word from leadership...that is desperately needed right now to calm what remains of this nation. Until then, stand ready, find shelter and sanctuary where you can, and..."

Veronica snorted. "*Highly defensible* my ass! There's no such thing as highly defensible against these things."

"Do you really think the president is down? The first zombie president?"

"I don't know. I can't think about it."

"Wait, listen!" Alex turned up the radio as new information poured from the speaker.

"...D.C. has been overrun, has fallen...Repeat: the government in Washington, D.C. has fallen, including the White House and the Capitol Building. Other major cities have also gone dark: New York, Boston, Atlanta, Miami, Chicago... Incoming reports also have a battle raging now in Los Angeles. It was thought that the west coast might be safer…"

"Atlanta," Veronica said glumly.

"Look around the plane," Alex said in a monotone voice, a command just coming without conscious thought. "See what kind of useful gear you can scrounge up. Flare gun, first aid kit, flashlight, tools, anything."

Veronica undid her seatbelt catch and started rooting around the plane while the radio bulletin continued.

"Although the outbreak of this unknown disease-causing agent, responsible for violent, irrational behavior reminiscent of fictional zombies, is widespread in the major cities, there are reported to be survivors barricading themselves inside at numerous locations within the fallen areas…"

Alex was jarred from the broadcast by Veronica's yell. "I've got something! Two things!"

He heard her dragging something forward over the cabin seats.

"What you got?"

A flashlight landed on her empty front seat.

"Okay. And?"

She tossed two backpacks up front. Alex's eyes widened immediately as he recognized what they were.

"Parachute packs. Hmmmm…."

"What do you think?"

"I've jumped a couple dozen times. You?"

"Never. How hard can it be? Put it on, jump out, wait a few seconds to clear the plane and then pull this cord here, right?" She pointed to a pull cord at the bottom of one of the packs.

"That's pretty much it. Now that I think of it, it's not a bad idea. Even if I could pull off a controlled landing with this thing, it's going to be damn near impossible to get close to the CDC headquarters, assuming we can commandeer a vehicle and we aren't immediately eaten by airport zombie security."

Veronica nodded. "Screw it. Let's jump. I know how to open the door already, at least."

"Yeah, but what then? Assuming this doctor's even still alive, barricaded or whatever, and assuming we can get to her without being eaten, how do we get her out of a city overrun with millions of flesh-eating monsters?"

"One thing at a time, please." Veronica tried to smile as she slipped an arm through one of her parachute straps. "Try to focus, will you?"

After a less-than-graceful circling of the major city hub, Alex figured out how to put the plane into autopilot for a somewhat lower altitude as they flew back around the outskirts of Atlanta and plotted a straight bath toward the taller buildings and where they mapped the CDC center. "We should jump now before we get too close to the heart of the city. Hopefully when the plane crashes it'll provide a distraction without killing innocent people."

Veronica donned her 'chute pack while Alex made final adjustments to the plane's controls, slowing the airspeed down to just above a stall, before doing the same. He scoured the ground, a few thousand feet below.

"Ready?" He grabbed the flashlight from the seat and shoved it into a pocket of his jeans. "Remember, flex your knees and roll when you land. Can't afford either of us to have a sprained ankle or worse. You first."

Veronica gripped his hand and looked into his eyes. Then she slid across the seat and gripped the door latch again. "Here goes nothing."

She pushed the door open and dangled her feet outside while they felt and heard the rush of air.

"On three!" Alex counted it down. "...jump!"

Veronica dropped away from the plane. Alex watched to make sure she wouldn't hang up on any part of the aircraft, and then he launched himself into the air after her. For a few heartbreaking moments, it seemed like she wasn't going to open her chute. Was there some problem with it? She had just found these laying around, basically. What if they had some defects?

Then, just as he wondered if he could go into a steep dive and catch up to her before deploying his own chute to slow them both, he saw a white petal bloom in the air beneath him, and Veronica was jerked skyward for a few seconds before drifting gently back downward.

Alex pulled the ripcord for his 'chute and smiled when it opened. *Enjoy the ride.*

And he did, gliding and swaying gracefully, feeling the wind and the ultimate peace and silence…until they came within a few hundred feet of the ground and saw what they were dropping into.

25.

CDC Headquarters, Atlanta, Georgia

Dr. Arcadia Grey stared helplessly at a cage full of rhesus macaque monkeys, every one of which was dead with an iron spike through its head after having been stunned with a captive bolt pistol. In a separate cage, a single, perfectly healthy specimen—the last such example she had access to—perched on a wooden dowel, rocking uneasily back and forth.

Grey's hands trembled with impotent rage as sweat beaded on her high forehead, above which black hair strewn with silver streaks poured down her back in a ponytail.

Working from Xander Dyson's research materials created in the days leading up to his untimely death on Adranos Island, she had thrown everything she could think of at the prion infection. Everything. But so far to no avail whatsoever. She hadn't made any headway on it, other than eliminating the techniques she had tried. It didn't help having a room full of concerned scientists and political leaders watching her every move, either. Call it scientific stage fright, but she wasn't used to working with so many pairs of eyes on her at once. Usually she was the boss, directing her contingent of junior scientists, researchers and lab assistants, but the truth was that right now there weren't really too many safe places to go, and those present wanted to get the news of an antidote or vaccine firsthand, since getting reliable information was fast becoming a difficult proposition in the wake of the rapid societal breakdown.

Presently, a video monitor mounted on the wall came to life with an image of a harried-looking President of the United States, with Arcadia visible in an inset window, a reminder that she was visible to the president as a disheveled mad scientist in front of a cage of dead monkeys.

"Dr. Grey, I need an update on the research, but first tell me, is it still safe in your building?"

She took a deep breath and straightened as she addressed the Commander-in-Chief. The others in the room looked on with rapt attention as well.

"My floor is on lockdown, Mr. President, and is safe for the moment, although the sounds coming from outside are most... disconcerting. I think the upper floors have been overrun."

"I promise I'll do what I can to shore up defenses around you as soon as this call ends."

That promise didn't have much of a ring of certainty around it, she thought. *He's scared.*

"Now, I apologize for being so brusque, but I fear I don't have much time. What progress have you made?"

"I'll be blunt myself, Mr. President. I've been pursuing what I hoped would be leads from research notes of the late Dr. Xander Dyson, but so far nothing has been effective. There are still further avenues for me to try, but the biggest wall I'm running up against now is that I only have one more monkey, and no way to get more test subjects."

"Mice? Rats?"

"Different physiology. Wouldn't be helpful." She turned and pointed to the still-living macaque behind her. It bared its teeth in the direction of the camera. "Without more testing, I can't run other scenarios and try modifications to work on humans. I really need..." She trailed off, scratching her head like it was an itch that would never go away. *I need a miracle...*

"As it turns out, I can help you with your specimen needs. I'll tell you more in a minute, but in all honesty, Dr. Grey, the way things are going here I doubt I'll even live to see the fruits of your labor."

Gasps issued from several in the room.

"Sir?" Grey was just as stunned.

"We're under heavy attack. Our military is putting up a fearsome defense but there is such a heavy concentration of enemy here I have to believe that whoever orchestrated this goddamned fucking apocalypse, pardon my French, targeted D.C. specifically as priority-one for annihilation. They know about our defenses, and the bunker I'm currently locked inside."

"Mr. President..." Arcadia had no idea what to say.

"It's okay." The president held a hand up as if to placate her. "The American people are resilient and resourceful. They'll get through this. I know they will. As for the government, rest assured that if our bunker here is breached, protocols are in place for continuity of government. Control will be handed out in the event that..." The president choked up for a moment.

Dr. Grey cleared her throat and moved the conversation forward. "Mr. President, you mentioned helping me with my experimental specimens?"

"Yes, yes!" His face brightened, seemingly glad to have something concrete to divert his mind from the disaster so close at hand. "Listen carefully. A CIA agent by the name of Veronica Winters and one of her associates is en route to your location as we speak via small aircraft to pick you up and take you to a research bunker set up in Colorado."

"Colorado?"

"Yes, but—" They could hear loud noises emanating from behind the president now—muffled explosions and shouting. He turned around quickly before facing the camera once more. "I need to get going, but listen: I'm told that we have animals suitable for your research in place in the Colorado facility along with a small research staff already there. I'm going to send you their contact information so that you can have them start preparing whatever you need while you are en route? Is that clear?"

"Yes, sir."

"Good. Make sure you bring any materials you require and can reasonably carry—computer files, specialized equipment..."

"Will do, Mr. President."

"Get to Colorado. Finish your work. This nation is counting on you."

"Of course, sir." She stood at attention, not sure if she should salute at such a momentous occasion, or bow?

"Oh, and Dr. Grey?"

"Yes, Mr. President?" She waited, expecting a grand motivating statement, a last inspirational word to define the struggle and create a turning point in the war.

Suddenly the screen flickered, a loud explosion was heard and black smoke began pouring into the room with the president.

"Mr. President?" The last thing she saw was his face awash in sheer terror.

Then the screen went black and stayed that way.

26.

Shadow Location Alpha —minutes earlier

William DeKirk grinned as he watched his compliment of wall-mounted monitors that fed him a steady diet of satellite driven real-time video. He was almost beside himself with ecstasy, finally witnessing the culmination of so much effort, planning and vision. The White House was burning. The Capitol Dome had been shattered. New Orleans had once again been turned into a city of lawlessness and ruin in the face of disaster. Every time he looked at a different screen, there was some wonderful view of annihilation playing out in a different locale.

He had done it… Dredged up a long-dormant biological agent from the frozen depths of a subterranean Antarctic lake and used it not only to reanimate dinosaurs and create human zombies, but to control them. It was almost too good to be real. Yet it was.

He picked up a device that superficially resembled a TV remote and clicked a few buttons in sequence, then watched on screen as a squadron of four pterodactyls abruptly turned in mid-air.

DeKirk's eyes flashed and he felt that primal hunger again, sensing the approach of living beings.

The doors opened and about three dozen men and women entered, hurrying inside. One of them said, "It's time. Communication coming through any moment."

DeKirk forced himself to keep his attention on the screens. The newcomers filed quickly inside and took seats around a large oval conference table. DeKirk finally stood, composed himself and turned to greet them. They nodded to acknowledge him and lowered their heads in mild deference.

That would change soon enough, he thought. They knew it, knew what was coming, but didn't realize the extent of it all yet. No one did except him.

A balding man with red eyes from sleeplessness or just downright horror, pointed at the largest of the video screens, where the view it had been depicting of Atlanta under siege flickered, dissolved into snow and then coalesced into a hi-def video chat with of the President of the United States. He was flanked by a cadre of high-ranking officials—cabinet members and Joint Chiefs of Staff. His face was the very picture of grim. On screen, the POTUS raised a hand to gain their attention, and then spoke.

"Ladies and gentlemen of the Springfield, Missouri Shadow Location Alpha. As you are no doubt aware, the unthinkable has come to pass. You may not have ever expected to be in this role, or you may have thought one of the other locations would be picked, but you have been entrusted with the continuation of the government of the United States of America—our great country—in the event that the primary government falls."

He leaned closer to the camera. "I am here to tell you, with the heaviest of hearts, that it has fallen." He paused to let that sink in and then continued. "By now, I'm sure you've seen the heartbreaking footage from our capital and other landmarks."

A table full of nodding heads uttered somber murmurs of "Yes, Mr. President," and then the POTUS went on again.

"Effective immediately, the government of the United States and all duties and responsibilities it encompasses have been transferred to you per the Continuity of Operations Plan. The future of our great nation lies in your hands, people. *Your* hands." He pointed at them through the lens.

From his desk, still seated apart from the main group, DeKirk tried to show no emotion, but it was difficult to not allow his face to light up like a child's on Christmas morning.

The shadow government had been enacted, and *he was a part of it!* No, fuck that, DeKirk thought. He *was* it. The president continued to speak to the group but DeKirk could no longer concentrate on the words, he was so giddy with feelings of accomplishment and rapture. He'd just been handed the keys to the kingdom.

Who would have thought?

While the former president droned on, DeKirk picked up his remote control. He pressed 9-1-1 and then held down Source for three seconds. An indicator light flashed red six times and DeKirk set the remote back down on his desk.

He stood and cleared his throat, then looked back to the group.

"Jorgenson. Mayweather. Daniels..." He called out a list of half a dozen names, most of those at the table shooting him dirty looks. *You're interrupting the president!* But one by one, and with great obedience, those whose names had been called rose from their seats and moved calmly but quickly to the other side of the room.

"What's going on?" the POTUS inquired. "Are you under attack there? Is everything secure?"

It was DeKirk's turn to take the limelight. Aware that he was on camera even from here, and finally in the camera's focus, he addressed the former president.

"Yes, Mr. President, we are under attack, and yes, everything is quite okay."

At that moment, a heavy rumbling noise was heard, growing louder by the second. By the time the heads of those still seated at the table had turned to look toward the room's entrance, where the sound was loudest, the door exploded in a hail of wood splinters as the head of a crylopholosaur smashed into the room.

Beyond the door, beyond the crylo, was an enormous underground facility: massive pillars, parked 18-wheelers, overhead lights and various off-shoot corridors leading to storage rooms, warehouses, greenhouses, databanks and all manner of highly secure vaults. The dinosaur, however, had been DeKirk's latest wildcard, brought in with the last round of supplies inside the trucks, and released at his command.

The president's cry of "Oh my God," was drowned out by the screams of terror issuing from his newly enacted shadow government. Except for seven of them, including DeKirk, who stood quietly on the other side of the room, wielding remote controls with knowing grins on their faces. Their day had finally come.

On the heels of the dinosaur came a dozen human zombies, wheezing and rasping with wet, mucous-laden breathing while they poured into the room and attacked those not under DeKirk's protection—his loyal followers. DeKirk became energized at the sight of his former colleagues being stripped of their flesh while still alive, being torn apart in the most brutal of ways, bones separated, blood spilled, organs consumed before their very eyes until the light in them changed.

The carnage caused DeKirk's own eyes to begin to turn yellow, but even among his own Inner Cabinet, there were some who didn't yet know, and now was not the optimal time for such a revelation. There was enough going on as it was.

Satisfied that the work at the table was well under control, DeKirk turned his attention back to the videoconference screen. He walked over to the camera so that he would be the full subject of the frame.

"Hello, Mr. President—sorry, that's not your title anymore, though, is it?"

The ex-president leaned forward. "All this time... *You.*"

DeKirk smiled. "Me. Do you know me now, have you guessed?"

The Shadow Government—a rotating crew selected by double-blind teams, replaced every two years. No one in current politics knew their identities. No one in fact, knew them at all, it was all handled with the utmost secrecy. Family, friends, colleagues, no one knew. Those sequestered could keep contact with the outside world, but only in sanitized messages or video feeds that were tailored to cover stories.

"*DeKirk,*" the ousted president said. "So that's why we couldn't find you these past few years."

Spreading his arms out wide, DeKirk smiled. "Guilty as charged. Hidden by your own people, right under your own noses. Irony is delicious, isn't it?"

"You maneuvered yourself into this position, got on the list."

"Guilty again," DeKirk admitted. "And once inside Camelot down here, it was all just a simple popularity party." He glanced around the blood and gore-splattered room, at the heaving crylo, panting and drooling blood like a satiated hound after a hunting expedition, at the seven men and women, heads bowed, meekly offering silent assent. "I've been chosen by my electorate down here, and now..." DeKirk laughed. "It's over, *sir.* You're looking at the new President of the United States."

A sudden commotion, and one of the women—not quite dead yet—scrambled from under the table, made a break for the door.

The crylo swung its reptilian head over the table and caught her in a flash. It chewed off the upper half of the woman in one bite, and the lower section flopped onto the table, legs still kicking. DeKirk gave a nod, activating the mental and pheremonal 'remote' in his brain, and the other undead went crazy attacking her remains. Two members of DeKirk's trusted shadow government flinched and turned from the sight, but the sounds were still beyond revolting.

"What in God's name?" the ex-president spat. "You're controlling them? You're..."

DeKirk sent the reptile on to the next victim, the last one trying to flee the room. In the aftermath, he returned his attention to the fallen president, who had retreated into the flickering shadows. "Yes, I'm controlling them. Just as I'm now officially in control of *us*. Both sides of this war are now under my control. I'll tell our forces where to go, what to attack and defend, and if I feel like it, I'll have them disarm, stand down and..." He licked his lips. "...just wait for the end."

The ex-president glared. "We'll stop you, DeKirk. We will..."

DeKirk tilted his head to one side as if considering the statement congenially, but his eyes flashed yellow. "I highly doubt that, and I have no idea who you mean by 'we'? Possibly our allies across the pond? The other world powers? Don't hold your breath, I have plans for them as well. In the meantime, don't expect this video feed to last. My first order of business will be to disrupt the communications satellites, to go dark with the exception of a few lines of communication only I'll control."

Without news, without the ability to coordinate, the fear and chaos would be augmented a hundred-fold. He wouldn't be able to shut down everything, but could knock out enough of them to cause the desired effect.

Suddenly, they all heard shouting come from the ex-president's end of the video chat. On screen, the ex-president looked over his shoulder as his people left his side and fled from something off camera but coming close, fast.

"Oh shoot," DeKirk said. "I thought I'd have more time to gloat." The screen flickered, and the ex-president was a blur, running for a back room, chased by a mob of undead... Then the screen went blank.

Sighing, DeKirk made a flicking motion with his finger that caused the crylo to retreat, back through the door and into the shadows of the larger bunker facility. The other undead, standing now, their meals finished, wobbled uncertainly, looking in his direction. Until he made a similar motion and they promptly obeyed, retreating out the door, single file.

DeKirk pulled out the main chair at the table, glanced back to the screens of devastation around the country, and let out a sigh.

"Gentlemen and ladies of my new cabinet. Congratulations on your positions. Now, sit, take a deep breath and relax. You've earned it. The hard part is over."

He smiled as they all took their seats.

"This next phase at least, is going to be a lot more fun."

Part 3: New World Order

27.

Alex lost sight of her chute in the mayhem, the smoke and the sea of bodies.

At first he thought they were both dead and they were landing straight in a crowd of undead, but then he breathed a sigh of relief—just before he hit ground and the air rushed out of him as a pair of guardsmen caught him.

"Hope you're not infected!" he grunted as he regained his balance.

"No," one of them said. "And we plan to damn well stay that way."

"Welcome to Atlanta," the other said, looking around the devastation and the eerily-quiet cityscape. "Such as it is."

Alex shook off the straps and wriggled out of the chute. "My friend, where is she?"

"Saw her strike the side of Peachtree Center and drop into those trees there." He pointed to a section of the street barely visible over the heads of more crowds and bottlenecked traffic.

Alex took stock of his surroundings. He saw several contingents of National Guard evacuating hundreds of people, masses carrying their children and a few precious possessions. Gunfire roared back a half mile from where they had been fleeing. He saw tanks and makeshift fences in that direction, a flimsy line of defense, but one that was holding—for now.

"We can't keep them back much longer," the one guard said as if reading his mind. "Too many side streets, and the buildings are infested. They're coming out the windows, leaping from six stories high, and fucking getting right up."

"Tell me about it," Alex said. "Ok, good luck. Get everyone as far away as you can."

"Then what?" asked the guard, again looking at the chute, then the sky, as if hoping Alex's miraculous arrival was like some angelic portent, a sign that divine help had arrived.

"Then you pray," Alex said, starting to head over to Peachtree Center, before calling back. "And tell me how to get to the CDC!"

#

Veronica found herself in a moment of panic, her legs dangling twenty feet over the ground where two zombies scampered, smelling her fear and her blood from the gash in her forehead where she must have hit the building wall before falling into the thorny and saving clutches of this tree. Her chute had caught, barely. One of the straps had torn loose, the other was sliding up her shoulder, and in another few inches she'd have nothing keeping her from dropping into the midst of the creatures that were even now leaping into the air, reaching higher than anyone should, but still coming up a few feet short.

It's not going to end like this, she thought. Not when we just got here.

She winced with the pain from her head and shook some blood out of her eye as she reached into her jacket pocket for the 9mm. Fumbled for it, but suddenly the tree shook just as she registered hearing breaking glass, some of which fell past her, slicing through leaves and off branches. Above her, something crashed and broke through branches, hissing and screeching, scrambling and desperately pushing through the foliage to get to her, having jumped out of a higher window.

"Oh you've got to be kidding!" Veronica pulled the gun free, tried to take aim, but the branches' motions and her precarious balance on the parachute strap caused her to swing back and fire wildly. The zombie thrashed and dug its way through the branches, gaining, reaching...

She fired again, thinking she couldn't miss, but just heard a sickening thump as the bullet went wide, maybe punching through the monster's shoulder. She fired four more shots, wildly blasting as she started spinning. Something had leapt high enough finally and caught her foot, yanking her down. The strap was about to break and the grasp on her ankle was beyond crushing.

Screaming, she looked down and aimed, fired—and this time didn't miss. The female zombie that had been trying to climb up her leg for a big bite suddenly had its skull punched through and brains scrambled. It dropped and landed on two other zombies.

Veronica swung her arm back around and aimed up. The other attacker's head thrust through the foliage, snarling and drooling blood. Those wicked yellow eyes locked on hers and as she swung back up after the weight's release, she aimed between them and squeezed the trigger.

Click.

Her heart sank, and the thing fell the last few feet onto her, claws out and mouth open with blood-stained teeth.

She had nowhere to duck, nothing to do except flinch, and pray...

Gunfire from below echoed at the same time she felt suddenly weightless.

Falling! Someone had shot her strap.

She turned in mid-air, saw a familiar face in the alley, then fell into a crowd of zombies.

#

With no time to think it through, Alex had two choices: shoot the tree-hugging zombie about to pounce on Veronica and risk the blood from the headshot getting in her mouth and eyes (whether or not that was the mode of transmission), or fire a volley over her shoulder, and blast through the chute strap holding her in place.

In hindsight, he should have shot the zombie, not realizing that having her fall out of its reach only meant that if she survived the drop, she'd be served up right in the midst of four other slavering monstrosities eager for their next meal.

Stupid! He thought it even as he held down the trigger on the M5. On the first swipe, he had the barrage cut through the restraints and set her free, but then he aimed lower and sideways, ripping the airborne zombie across his spine and hopefully up through its head, although he couldn't tell.

Then, still running, he shifted his aim, yelled ahead to distract the crowd, crouched and opened fire, sweeping left and right, at about head level. Fighting the recoil, he kept the automatic fire spitting out lethal violence, tearing through flesh and bone, skulls and jawbones. Teeth flying, shoulders and chests pierced.

"Veronica!"

He saw a leg kick out from the pile, sweeping two other pairs and toppling one attacker—a former national guardsman by the outfit. In a flash, Veronica was up on her knees and thrusting a knife into the zombie's forehead.

She screamed in the next instant as the tree-bound zombie fell right where she had been. Headfirst—what was left of its head, at least, after a random round from Alex's M5 struck home.

She got up, tenderly favoring one leg, but put some weight on the other, happy it held without much pain.

"Soft landing?" Alex asked, breathing hard, eyeing the fallen zombies for movement.

Veronica nodded. "Nice of them to break my fall." She glanced up and down her arms and legs, looking for bites. "Clean, too. Now..."

Suddenly another window shattered above and behind her, on the second floor, and a teen girl in all black with spiky hair leapt through, landing in a shower of glass two feet away from Veronica.

She flinched, but rolled her eyes at Alex, then shifted her grip on the knife handle, spun around and struck with sideways precision into the zombie's left temple just as the girl rose, snarling and about to leap.

Veronica's arm trembled, but she held the pose, locked in to the girl's skull until the ferocity in those yellow eyes dulled and the body went limp.

"Damn you're good," Alex said admiringly as she let the body drop and pulled out her knife.

"Not a skill I'd want to brag about on my resume. Unless the world's gone completely to shit."

Alex glanced around and back up to the building, expecting more windows to shatter any second, releasing more of the converted, who had until only this morning been normal work-going schleps, showing up to meetings or getting their coffees.

Now they were eating their colleagues and leaping out onto unsuspecting and incredulous people who still couldn't fathom what was happening.

A goddamn zombie apocalypse, Alex thought.

"Can there really be a way to stop all this?" he voiced, as distant explosions rocked the street, and the building shook and screams of the living and the shrieks of the dead echoed off the concrete corridors of Atlanta.

"Got to try," Veronica said, reloading her 9mm and eyeing his M5. "Any more of those?"

"No doubt we'll find 'em along the way," Alex said. "Lots of soldiers and National Guard among the converted. They've all been dropping their weapons for us."

Nodding, Veronica took his arm. "Thanks for the rescue, now let's go. Do you have any idea where we are?"

Alex motioned down a side alley. "I think so. Not the best with directions, and of course GPS is shot."

"Satellites are down?"

"Yeah." Alex had checked his smart phone along the way. Nothing but a spinning circle and a blank map. "Don't know if the system's just overloaded, the power's out, or if all cell service was jammed as part of the attack. So I had to do this the old fashioned way."

She gave him a sideways look. "You, a guy, actually asked for directions?"

"Don't start."

"Okay Mr. MapQuest, how long 'til our destination?"

They started off down the deserted alley, where smoke from an upstairs window billowed thick and black into the sky, blotting out the sun.

"If there aren't any distractions, maybe fifteen minutes."

"Distractions meaning ravenous zombies, flying mutated dinosaur corpses or—"

She stopped suddenly pulled back on his arm.

A shop—a Starbucks—in front of them on the corner of Peachtree Ave, at the end of the alley, crumbled into dust and debris, shattered concrete and blasted windows, just crushed by an enormous...

"Is that a foot?"

Veronica pulled him aside, into a doorway where they could just peer around the side.

Something made a horrific, warbling bellow, and then a dark form strode into view. Just a portion of the form—a body and a long twisted neck, and through the smoke rising from the crushed store, they caught just the hint of a huge horned skull and wicked jaws opening and snapping at the air. A head that moved this way and that, as frightening dragon-like eyes sought out prey in every direction.

Veronica's whisper was barely audible. "Dear God, what the hell is that?"

"That," Alex said, "is the freakin' largest dinosaur ever discovered. A dreadnought. Thought to be larger, heavier and more frightening that a *T.rex*, although... fortunately not carnivorous, and this one doesn't look as big as they could get."

"What? Then... wait, it sure looks like it wants to eat us."

"I'd say with this virus prion thing, all bets are off. It may not have the razor sharp teeth of a *T. rex*, but what it does have, coupled with its size, speed and ridiculous hunger, can more than make up for its former vegetarianism."

"Great. DeKirk really brought in the muscle."

"Right, as it's doubtful this thing is going to leave many people alive after being chomped on, not to be transformed. So it's here for intimidation, and pure destruction."

"Or a distraction," Veronica guessed, hearing helicopters somewhere up there, and hoping they were fully armed with an array of missiles.

The hulking behemoth grumbled, bellowed a cry up to the sky as it tilted its head, then it continued on its path, picking up speed toward the sound of desperate, sporadic gunfire. Someone was giving it a valiant go out there.

"Not our fight right now," Alex said. "We've got a mission."

"True," Veronica said as she watched the last of the dreadnought lumber by and noticed several humanoid forms clinging to its hind quarters, even grasping on to the enormous tail as it swayed back and forth, knocking over street lights and breaking storefront windows. "Stay on target."

28.

Washington, D.C.

Major Remington, along with a force of six—all that remained from the defenders of Pennsylvania Avenue—including the shell-shocked radar technician with barely any combat experience—left the tank and ascended the steps to the East Wing of the White House Complex with a cautious expectation of dread.

They looked to the left, to the main building, half in ruins, with flames licking out from the upper balcony windows. The second leftmost pillar was shattered by a stray 120mm round, and all the windows to the East Room were broken. Fire raged from the drapes inside, where screams punctuated the crackling fire.

The president would have been escorted to the PEOC—the President's Emergency Operations Center—a bunker designed by FDR, below the attached East Wing and behind ten feet of reinforced concrete, designed to withstand all but a direct nuclear hit.

Remington paused at the top of the stairs, right hand raised in a fist to stop the others. He took a moment and looked up at the smoke-filled sky, where no more air support was in sight, and a lone ptero circled aimlessly as if awaiting orders, perhaps to see how they fared inside. At their backs, the barricades had broken, and a swarm of zombies pushed through, most continuing on the avenue, a few sniffing the air, hearing the screams, and heading this way.

"About to have company," Remington said, turning back to the front door, which was broken on its hinges, leaning open. "This may be a one-way trip, but we have our orders. Get down to the bunker, clear the path and secure the POTUS. Marcus and Harrison: get up to level two and man the turrets, buy us some time."

White House defenses were up there, but whoever operated them was likely dead or transformed, and Remington didn't have a lot of confidence that those two brave men rushing in ahead of him, firing a few rounds on their way to the stairs, had any chance of survival.

Do any of us?

He brushed off the thought, but then had a passing moment's reflection of his daughter, back home in Kansas. He wouldn't let himself wonder at her fate, only hoping that the contagion hadn't spread anywhere near there, and if possible, a miracle would save her before then. If not...

He clamped down on the line of thought. They were coming, and fast. Shrieking, hissing, starving, racing up the stairs toward them.

The undead.

He rushed in, leading his men, with just a fading image of his daughter's smiling eyes in his mind before visions of true Hell took her place.

#

The next minutes were a blur of mind-numbing violence, of shocking visuals and utter fear as Remington's team went from the lobby to the hall to the East Room, clearing the way of former aides and hapless tourists who had been in the wrong place at the wrong time. There was a moment of heart-wrenching grief as they discovered a group of school kids and their teacher holed up in a pantry beside the kitchen, cowering for their lives until they saw Remington as a savior.

He was anything but that now, though, and insisted they stay put, stay hidden and quiet. His was another mission, and in all likelihood, this poor group would never make it out alive. If he secured the president and somehow reinforcements arrived to retake the capitol, there might be a chance for them, but for now he had to press on.

Into the East Wing lobby, where three zombies—former secret service by the look of their suits and the dark glasses one of them still wore—feasted on the body of what might have been the press secretary. They looked up from their meal, snarling with bloody lips, and leapt onto the dining room table. Remington aimed, but never fired, as the radar tech let loose with a hail of bullets from his procured M5, raking the fiends wildly from neck to torso, a few shots in the barrage hitting home, splitting their heads and puncturing brains.

All three zombies went down, and as Remington, with newfound respect for the radar tech, led the men around the table to the far hall, he fired a mercy shot into the brain of the still-twitching secretary.

Wordlessly, grouped in a tight circle, heads on a swivel and covering every angle, they moved into the hallway, through a door and to the elevator leading down to the bunker.

#

When the doors opened and he and his soldiers filed into the hallway, Remington's worst suspicions were confirmed. The door to the command center, the massive entrance to the unbreakable bunker, was open. Ajar like someone had just left the back door open.

First, he locked and held the elevator at this level so it wouldn't rise again for anybody or anything else, then he led his men down the darkened corridor, stepping over bodies as they went. The marines and secret service had certainly put up a fight, he thought, admiring a multitude of headshot kills, the zombie bodies piling up as they approached the open door and the flickering light within.

Something sparked inside, and a wet shuffling sound filtered out. Remington held up a fist, then scanned the faces of his men. He saw their desperation, their fear, as he heard that sound again from inside, chilling like a throaty rattle, like an animal having difficulty swallowing a still-twitching meal.

Remington turned sideways and eased inside the command center bunker. A light above the main oblong table flickered as another one sparked in a regular rhythm. Bodies were everywhere, draped over tables and chairs, but not as many as Remington would have expected. Did they not have time to evacuate enough of the senior staff and officers? Did the president even make it down here?

Someone bumped him from behind, then pointed behind a section of shattered monitors and a hanging screen with dangling wires. A hunched form on the ground, someone in a dark blue suit, slicked back grey hair. Face... face down in the neck of a female form. A white blouse stained crimson. Narrow legs, one foot still in a black high heel, the other bare—and partially chewed, the white bones sticking out.

"Is that...?" The radar tech stepped forward, craning his neck.

Remington reached out to hold him back.

"Sir?"

"Quiet," Remington hissed. He tried to pull him back, but he was already moving.

"Mr. President?"

Remington leveled his gun, trying to get a shot. He didn't know if it was the Commander-in-Chief or not, but there was no way anybody here was still human.

"This was a mistake," someone said at his back.

"We're screwed," another spoke, echoing the voice in Remington's head. This was indeed quite probably a one-way trip, but Remington had hoped at least they could hold out in the bunker, support the president and perhaps mount a counter-offensive from this command center. Now...

Now the former president raised his head, and a mass of stringy flesh—that had just been part of his wife's throat—hung from his teeth before he wildly sucked the grizzled strips into his mouth and down his throat.

A meaty snarl as those yellow eyes scanned the company.

"Mr. President!" shouted the radar tech, and Remington had the sense that despite everything he'd just been through, the tech was somehow in awe of meeting his ultimate commander, and it was clouding all reason.

Remington aimed. "Get down, son."

He turned, then stepped in the path of the president, like a secret service agent having spotted an assassin.

"No, I can't let you take that shot. He's—"

"Not your president, idiot! Get down."

For an instant, he had a shot, just as President Zombie stood, and his neck lolled to one side so Remington got a clear look down his sights, right between those yellow eyes—eyes that only hours earlier had been privy to the nation's deepest secrets...

But just then the rubble to their left exploded with two forms that scrambled out from the debris and launched themselves across the room. One slammed into the man behind Remington, catching him completely off-guard, while the other, a little slower, running on a stump that had been blown off in a grenade blast— stumbled right into a barrage of bullets from the others.

Remington spun and fired into the shadows, seeing more movement near the back, toward the adjoining room and the connecting facilities, the kitchen and restrooms that they hadn't had a chance yet to clear out.

How many back there?

A scream and the radar tech went down, toppled and nearly bent in half. Remington heard a crack as loud as another gunshot, the man's spine snapping as the president leapt on him, broke him backwards and fastened his jaws on the soft tissue of his neck.

"Damn it!" Remington spun back around and aimed, trying to get a clear shot through the mayhem of the other men running and firing and trying to stay away from the zombies, the former president's staff. A man just barely recognizable as the vice president lurched across his field of vision, and this time Remington didn't hesitate.

One shot to the temple, and that annoying prick who'd killed the last defense spending bill went down in a bloody heap. Remington stepped over the body, just as one of his commandos shot down a zombie attacking from his back. He sighted at the blurry crimson mess of the president and the radar tech, trying to get a clear head shot, but then—as the president looked up at him through a haze of insatiable hunger—Remington realized it didn't matter. They were both gone.

Lost, just like everyone upstairs and in the Capitol. Like everyone out there on the avenue. Like all his friends and mates he trained with, flew with and ate and drank with. Like everyone he had ever known and…God help them all… everyone he had ever loved.

He shut his eyes.

And held down the trigger, steeling against the recoil, feeling every cartridge loosed by his weapon firing out, finding its mark or not, he didn't care. Enough of the rounds would, and that's all that mattered.

Because really, nothing mattered. It didn't matter that he was killing a man who had only moments earlier been fighting not just for his life, but for a very way of life, holding on to an existence grounded in logic and safety and the pursuit of peace. It didn't matter that he was destroying another man who had earlier been the leader of the free world, the sole person who could rally a nation in defense, order a wholesale retaliation and lead other world powers into some sort of counter-offensive.

It didn't matter because now everything was lost.

Remington opened his eyes to gaze with no satisfaction whatsoever upon the results of his work.

The two bodies cut to ribbons, holes torn through skulls and chests, brains and gore streaked across the tiled floor to the concrete wall.

Breathing calmly (because nothing mattered anymore, no need to get upset), Remington stepped over the remnants of the president. He walked through the remaining three commandos, all either still firing or locked in hand-to-hand combat with zombies. He made his way to the far edge of the room, where a TV screen hung more or less still intact, if a bit spattered with blood.

He approached the screen, dimly hearing two final gunshots behind him and the sound of bodies falling in a squishy heap. Approached the visual of a gray-haired man sitting calmly at a table, with several other distinguished men and women, who appeared to be calm and in control, if not a bit shell-shocked. The gray-haired man, a little-wild eyed, had a contented smile on his face that Remington thought more than out of place, given the general tone of the unfolding apocalypse.

"Hello there, major," said the man in a calm, assured voice as his eyes glanced around the bunker behind Remington. "Did I just witness you shooting the president in the head?"

"Former president," Remington said hollowly. "Who are you?"

The man grinned, licked his lips and Remington saw behind him the seal of the United States, along with a pair of U.S. flags at the back of the room, a room which seemed to have experienced its own share of mayhem.

"Quite right you are about that being the former president. You'll find I've been transferred all necessary codes, authority and security clearances, and as of..." He glanced at his watch. "...oh, about ten minutes ago, I'm your new Commander-in-Chief. I'm sending you verification of the transfer of power now."

Remington's eyes opened wide in surprise. Things were even more severe than he'd thought if the succession of government plan had already been enacted. He glanced over at his communication specialist and saw that he was already on his hand-held device, busy tapping the screen to verify that the incoming stream of encrypted codes matched what they had been given. Remington would not let his guard down and would have asked for the authentication string had DeKirk not offered it, but he was glad he did.

He heard a series of tones out of the technician's device and then the specialist gave him the thumbs up. "Authentication verified, sir. It's legit."

Remington nodded to the new commander. "Verification codes received and authenticated. I wish it were under better circumstances but I look forward to serving under your command all the same, President?..."

Remington swallowed hard and followed his three surviving men a moment later in standing to attention and saluting.

"President William DeKirk," the man said, standing and straightening his suit coat. "Now, kindly debrief me on the situation there at the White House. Because from where I'm standing..."

Remington narrowed his eyes, trying to see anything that would give an indication of where exactly these men and women were situated. Raven Rock? That would be Pennsylvania, but maybe it was the alternate bunker, rumored to be somewhere in Missouri. Or else Colorado, possibly?

"...it seems things aren't going too well there."

Remington put his hand down at his side, lifting the M5. "No sir, they are not. The Capitol is in flames, and the White House...severely compromised. The whole city..."

"I understand," the new president said. He leaned in until his face—and those oddly-tinted eyes loomed large on the screen.

"Now listen close, I'll tell you what I'd like you to do."

29.

Atlanta, CDC Headquarters

Alex ran up to the outside of the curved glass and steel building with Veronica a few steps behind him, wheeling on her heels as she swept the barrel of her gun across the landscape behind her. He pulled on the big handles of the double glass doors but they didn't budge. Locked.

He pressed his face up against the glass and looked inside to the lobby. The receptionist desk was unstaffed, potted plants knocked over, their dirt marring the white tile floor. A dead security guard, bullet hole smack in the middle of his forehead, lay sprawled in the middle of the room. Alex saw no one...or no thing...living. He took a step back and looked up at the towering facade.

Dr. Arcadia Grey was in there somewhere and it was his and Veronica's job to find her and bring her to the secret lab in Colorado. She was the best chance anyone had at developing an antidote. But how to get in?

"Intercom panel, over there!" Veronica pointed before spinning back around to fire a couple of shots at a distant zombie. Alex ran to the panel. He ran a finger along the directory that accompanied the buttons, seeking Grey's name...not there, but the Inquiries option was available.

He depressed the button and heard a ridiculously pleasant-sounding chime given the circumstances. Waited for an answer. After nearly a minute during which he hit the button several times, he was about to give up and try some other buttons to see if he could reach anyone, when a tired-sounding female voice issued from the speaker.

"Yes?"

Alex didn't think that was a proper government employee greeting, but it just went to show how far everything normal had been tossed out the window. He leaned in close to the speaker.

"Doctor Grey?"

"Who wants to know?"

He looked back at Veronica, who paused her lookout duties to monitor the conversation. He waved her over and then turned back to the speaker while she ran over to join him.

"My name is Alex Ramirez. I'm here with CIA Agent Veronica Winters. We were ordered here by the president to take you to a research lab in Co—"

"Alex!" Veronica put a finger across her lips, warning him not to divulge the location of the clandestine laboratory. She pulled his finger from the intercom button.

"Who knows who's listening in or if that's even her?"

The voice on the other end seemed to sense their concerns.

"Yes, it's me, Dr. Grey, and I was told to expect you. I know your plans for me, but listen, I can't leave."

"Why not?" Alex frowned. Other than the obvious: that maybe she was trapped in there, why else would she fight extraction?

"There's no point. If I don't figure this out fast, by the time we get to Colorado and start all over again there, it might be too late. For all of us. The things I need…they're all here."

Veronica stepped up to the intercom. "Doctor Grey, this is Agent Winters. I was told you'd have everything you needed with you in your lab, and you could transport them with us. Is that not the case?"

"That is indeed not the case. I need something else, there's a chance with the right specimen that I could figure this out here and now."

"What specimen?"

A pause ensued during which Alex wondered if the researcher was either afraid to say, or not allowed. "A live zombie. Or as alive as that term implies." She let that sink in for a moment while Alex and Veronica exchanged bewildered stares.

Dr. Grey continued. "Human or dinosaur, whichever you can get. Although I imagine the former would be easier to procure."

Alex spoke into the microphone while mentally picturing wrestling a crylopholosaur into submission. "Yeah, I vote for the human variety." But no sooner had he said it than he realized that, too, was extremely problematic.

"Hold on just a minute." Veronica's features were twisted into an angry mask. "You expect us to capture one of those disease carrying things and bring it back here?"

Dr. Grey's reply was quick in coming and earnest in tone. "My research is at a dead end without a live specimen. Believe me, I'm not looking forward to spending time in close proximity to one of them in the lab myself, but that's what has to be done if I'm put a stop to this thing one and for all. You want in to this place? Come back with a zombie."

#

"I can't believe she wouldn't give us so much as a tranquilizer dart," Veronica complained. "Or a net-gun, or just a net...something! How are we supposed to catch one of these things?"

She and Alex stood on a downtown street some distance from the CDC building, looking for a zombie to catch alive.

Alex put a hand on her shoulder, an attempt to calm her fraying nerves. "Maybe she doesn't have any, or maybe drugs would mess up her research. Who knows if tranqs would even work on their messed up physiology? She told us what we have to do. Let's do it and get out of here."

Veronica took a deep breath and held his gaze. "Okay. But how? How do we get one of those things back to the CDC building without it being able to bite or scratch?"

Alex took in their surroundings. They stood in a business area with office buildings behind them and in front of them what looked like a retail district with stores and shops. He pointed that way. "Think there's some stores up ahead. Let's see if we can find anything useful."

They set off down the block. It was deserted until they reached the beginning of the storefront section, where they were immediately confronted with four zombies stepping out of an alcove entrance to a woman's clothing boutique. Veronica gave the first two double-taps to the forehead with her pistol, but one of the other two leapt on her, seeking purchase with its teeth. At the same time, the other one attacked Alex. He gave it a violent kick and it flew back into the alcove where it slumped on the ground, legs at a weird angle. It stayed there, trying to move but unable for the moment to get up.

By the time he could turn his attention to Veronica, she was flat on her back on the ground, kicking the living dead woman off of her. As it stumbled backwards and then steadied itself, preparing for another assault, Alex took aim and put a shot between its eyes. The she-zombie dropped, dead for real. Veronica got to her feet and dusted herself off. Alex wasted no time.

"C'mon, let's see what's up here."

Alex and Veronica made their way down the row of stores. Most of them were clothing, one specializing only in hats. Finally, nearing the end of the block, they found some different types of shops. A now useless Sprint store. A frozen yogurt shop.

"Here we go!" Alex pointed at the last business on the block, a sporting goods franchise.

"Hardly the time for fun and games."

"Let's just see what's in there. I have an idea."

The store was closed and by the looks of things with no one inside. Alex tried the door. Locked. Peering inside the display window which featured mannequins in various athletic dress, swinging bats and holding footballs, it looked to Alex like the place was left in a hurry but hadn't yet been looted or the scene of a major battle.

He held his pistol by the barrel and smashed the window with the butt. He kicked away some more of the glass until they could easily pass through. Stepping inside the store, he told Veronica, "Look for anything we might use to keep one from biting and to contain its hands."

She set off down an aisle, a doubtful look on her face as she glanced at racks of hiking gear—backpacks, water bottles, boots. She stopped in front of one of the packs, shrugged, and put it on. "Nice color. Wonder if they take Discover Card."

Two aisles over, Alex was checking out the hockey gear: sticks, pucks, pads, and goalie masks. *A helmet...* He took a closer look at them, picked one up. It was a sleek, tapered affair made of heavy-duty plastic with a slick paintjob—long canines on the forehead sticking down and on the chin guard sticking up, giving the impression that the player's entire face was a gaping maw of doom. The one he chose was a full helmet style and not simply a mask.

He held it up to his face, noting how the chin guard extended up to cover the entire mouth, with a plastic grill covering the face. Even better, a large, clear plastic deflector plate, meant to deflect high speed pucks, covered the entire mouth area.

Perfect!

He put it on and went to find Veronica. She was wandering the exercise equipment section, and for a brief second Alex felt like they were just an ordinary couple goofing around on a little shopping trip. Then he recalled the purpose of the hockey mask and the moment was gone.

"Hey, check this out!" She turned to look at him and a scream escaped her lips at the sight of him in the mask.

"Don't shoot! Geez, it's only me!"

"Damn it, Alex! You scared the crap outta me! As if that doesn't happen enough, the way things are lately."

He took the mask off and held it. "Sorry. Just wanted to show you the plan."

"What plan?"

"This." He held up the mask to his face and made snapping motions with his teeth by way of explanation.

Realization lit in Veronica's eyes and a smile took hold. "Not sure how we'll get it on one's head, but okay. I'm with you."

"We just need something for the hands. Keep looking."

One aisle over, Alex found the baseball stuff. He grabbed two large adult catcher's mitts and tried them on. They were both lefties but then he found a right-handed glove too and was satisfied that they would prevent a zombie from inflicting serious damage with its hands.

He found Veronica still in the exercise aisle, where she had removed a long section of sturdy elastic from a resistance trainer and showed it to Alex. He nodded.

"Let's go get our volunteer."

#

Sporting goods in tow, Alex and Veronica made their way back down the block. Now that they were ready, the street seemed to be devoid of undead, except for a lone crylo shuffling down the road, but they did nothing to incite it and it ambled away, head rooting at the ground. When they reached the woman's clothing store, Alex looked inside and saw the zombie he had fought with earlier still there in the entrance alcove, along with the lifeless bodies of its three comrades.

"That's our man."

Alex studied their target. It roamed around the alcove, apparently confused about how to get out or which way to go, stumbling once over the body of one of its fallen brethren.

"So how are we going to do this?"

"Very carefully."

"Seriously."

Alex concentrated on the zombie for a moment longer. "How about I place the gear on it but you hold the arms down? When that's done, you tie the elastic band around it for a leash."

Veronica unsheathed her big knife. "Why don't I just cut the thing's arms off, then we don't have to worry about that, at least."

"Dr. Grey said she wanted the specimen whole. That would mean with hands, and I don't want to come back and try this all again. Do it right the first time, my grandma always used to say."

Veronica shrugged. "Whatever. Grey better be able to do something with this thing is all I can say. Let's get it over with."

The zombie-fighting duo advanced on the alcove.

They split up, with Alex circling to the rear of the zombie—a tight fit against the storefront window—and Veronica stretched the piece of elastic out in front of her, testing it, looking for an opportunity.

The undead human focused its limited attention on Veronica, swiping at her with its arms. It reached for her, a weird groan coming from deep within its core, but she evaded its contact. Then, as it brought its arms up in another swing, Veronica used both of her own arms to wrap the elastic cord around the zombie's wrists, trapping them against one another.

At the same time, Alex slammed the hockey helmet down on the dumb brute's head, mashing it in place.

"Wrap those arms tight!"

Veronica wound the strap around the specimen's arms a couple of more times, then cinched it tight. Alex pounded the helmet down one more time to make certain it would stay put and then stepped back to admire his handiwork.

Ironically, the mythic beast imagery airbrushed onto the goalie mask, designed to elicit ferocity and to intimidate opponents, was infinitely less scary than the sight of the actual zombie's face, with its rot, ruin, and general suggestion of just how bad things could really get.

"That's quite an improvement, right?" Veronica remarked after quickly backing away. A row of gleaming, sharp teeth appeared white and healthy above the undead thing's real decayed stumps, while a pair of electric blue cat's eyes stood out in vivid contrast to the zombie's dull stare.

"Definitely."

Alex appraised the specimen momentarily. "Okay. Now for the hands."

Veronica held onto the slack elastic to control the thing's arms while Alex readied the catcher's mitt for the right hand. Veronica pulled the zombie's arms down and Alex kneeled by the hands. The helmeted head of the monstrosity lunged at Alex's neck, and he could hear it gnashing and slavering behind the mask, but it could not bite.

He slid the baseball glove on its right hand and wrapped a Velcro strap tight.

"New one, incoming!" Veronica pointed behind them where another zombie moved toward them. "Hold on!" She blasted the top of its skull open with her firearm and it dropped dead, its cranial contents running into a storm drain.

"One more glove!" Alex prepared the left baseball mitt while Veronica got control of the elastic again. They moved in and Alex crammed the glove onto the zombie's other hand, cinching it down as before. "Play ball!" Then he stepped away and admired his handiwork.

The zombie prisoner looked ridiculous, wearing a garish hockey mask with a professional leather catcher's mitt on each hand, while its arms were bound together in front of it with a piece of elastic, the free end of which was held by Veronica.

Alex pointed toward the CDC Headquarters building. "Okay, let's go, Sports Fan!"

30.

Washington, D.C. – PEOC

"Sir, if we want to have any chance of getting out of here, we have to leave now."

Remington ignored the other commando. He was aware of everything in this bunker—the three soldiers he had left, the sixteen-plus corpses, half of them partially-devoured, the rest with their heads blown off, the screens, some demolished and others showing either news feeds of the mayhem around the country or the scene outside captured by the closed circuit cameras—but his primary focus was on the man at the other end of the video feed.

"Mr. President..."

"DeKirk," the other man said with a glint in his eye as he backed away slightly and again the room filled the screen. Remington noted blood stains on the walls, gore streaking the tabletop and what looked like something large and hulking moving outside, in the doorway, perhaps guarding it.

What the hell happened there? And what was he dealing with? A budding sense of dread and hopelessness rose in his chest. *Could he elicit an answer and get to the truth?* "What's your situation, there, sir? Do you require assistance?"

"Under control for the moment, major, and much better than your situation, I wager."

Remington chewed his lip and eyed the closed circuit monitor. A herd of crylos stampeded across the White House lawn, while zombie pileups here and there indicated the recently deceased. DeKirk was right, things had deteriorated rapidly up there. *Was there an escape route down here?* There had to be, but he didn't know the layout or have any blueprints. *First things first.*

He turned to the closest aide and whispered, "Clear the bunker and look for an alternate exit."

"Good thinking, major," said DeKirk, and Remington lifted his eyes. *Great hearing or was this place just that wired up?*

"Sir... Mr. President." Remington stood at attention again. "Orders? Can you give me a status update? I assume you have full access there, as protocols have been transferred. Do you have links to the Air Force? To NORAD, to NATO? Europe? Are they offering assistance? Or are they facing something similar?"

DeKirk raised a hand motioning restraint. "Easy. From our initial reports, this…outbreak of madness has mostly been limited to the U.S. eastern seaboard and the gulf states."

"Outbreak of madness? Is that what we're calling it?"

DeKirk smiled and shrugged. "For lack of a more dramatic…and Hollywood fright night kind of term."

"Call 'em zombies," said one of the remaining commandos.

"And fuckin' dinosaurs from the grave," muttered another.

"Yes," DeKirk said, "I've heard the reports and…seen wondrous sights."

Wondrous? Remington repressed a shudder, again unable to take his eyes off DeKirk's oddly-hued pupils.

"Tell me, major. What would you suggest for our next course of action?"

He swallowed hard, tasting dust and blood and smoke. "Contact NATO, or mobilize our carriers overseas and activate the divisions supporting Germany and Korea, organize a coalition of other nations, stop the outbreak first from spreading overseas. I assume all flights are grounded. Then consider quarantines of…hell, the entire Mid-Atlantic states, maybe use the Mississippi as the dividing line, and…"

"We have new reports in from Los Angeles," said DeKirk in a less-than-sullen tone.

A lump lodged in his throat. "What reports?"

"Overrun with the infected. It happens fast, as you I'm sure you know well by now."

Remington lowered his eyes. "Then…"

"We're working on it," DeKirk said. "And yes, NATO will be our next call. I imagine they're pissing their pants right about now. Phones ringing off the hook upstairs, if you could get up there, with no response obviously. But we can't leave them waiting, we'll get in touch."

A hundred scenarios swarmed in Remington's mind, all revolving around how to protect the heartland, to set up defensible zones and perimeters of safety, to find some way to save the survivors (including his own family, hopefully) and mitigate the damage still to come.

"Tell him," said the commando at his back, "about the other mission."

Remington's eyes darted to him in a warning, but it was too late.

"Mission?" DeKirk leaned forward. "Yes, tell me, major. Or marine...I'm eager to hear of any other last minute strategies my predecessor may have deemed worthy. I am learning on the job, so to speak. First day and all."

Remington met the look of his soldier. *Damn. No choice, but were his fears unfounded?* He knew nothing of this DeKirk, this man suddenly thrust into power and given all the keys to the country, whatever that may be worth at the moment. Was he just some schlep groomed and kept ready in case the impossible happened? Or was there more to it? Even though he mentioned being new on the job—a job that would have any reasonable person stressed out beyond belief—he nevertheless seemed very calm and in control. *Something so not right about him,* as if none of this came as any surprise to him. *The man should be a puddle of absolute fear and loss, and yet he's cool as an icicle.*

He thought of his daughter, and everything again seemed to hang in the balance. *Don't tell him,* came her voice across the miles and down through the earth. *Don't, Daddy...*

"The CDC," said the commando, blurting it out as if the words were plucked right out of his throat. "The president...I mean the former president...sent an agent out on a mission."

"Atlanta?" DeKirk asked, raising an eyebrow. "Major, is this true?"

Remington returned his attention to the screen. *Don't tell.*

He had no choice. Cat was out of the bag. *But what could it matter?* "I only heard part of it, sir. Not sure the agent even got to the airport, she would have had to get through all the chaos, and..."

"She?" DeKirk leaned in. "That wouldn't be Agent Winters, now would it?"

Remington blinked. "Uh...sir, I think..."

"Thank you, major. So my predecessor sent the young agent with experience against these things down to the one place that might have... what...a cure? An antidote or vaccine?" He narrowed his eyes. "What was it, soldier?"

"I don't know, sir," said the commando, and Remington nodded, shrugging. "Only heard she was being sent there on a mission."

"An urgent mission, by the sounds of things." DeKirk turned and put his hands together behind his back. "Sounds like maybe I have a call to make before I respond to those Europeans."

Remington's lips dried out and felt like they were parched from days in the sun. "Sir, with all due respect..."

"That will be all," president DeKirk said, angling his head around so Remington could see the glint of yellow now, the irises changing, losing the battle to a hunger barely suppressed.

What the hell, was he...?

"Thank you for your information," DeKirk added, licking his lips. "I'll take care of things from here. I don't expect you'll make it out of there alive, but maybe someday I will see you again. In one form or another."

He reached forward, and before Remington could even think of a response, the screen went blank and left them in silence.

The silence of their tomb.

31.

CDC, Atlanta

Dr. Arcadia Grey had seen a lot of bizarre things in the last few hours, but she hadn't been prepared for the sight out the street entrance camera. The agent and the guy she was with from Washington were back, but not alone.

It reminded her of Halloween back home, looking out the front door and seeing a ludicrous costume, kids out-doing themselves for a good trick-or-treat performance. Except this time it was something far more severe, and the trick, if not avoided carefully, would be a nasty death. On the other hand, the treat was an antidote that could save all of humanity.

Once reasonably sure the specimen—a thrashing, zombified man with blood streaked down the front of his torn shirt, his wrists bound with some kind of elastic behind his back and his head covered like Jason from Friday the 13th in a hockey mask—was not going to break out and feast on the few survivors in here, Arcadia released the door locks and allowed them in.

Sealing the door behind them, she then spoke over the lobby intercom and directed Alex and Veronica to the east stairwell. Not trusting the elevators to continue operating reliably, and concerned about all manner of alternative entrance points for those monsters, perhaps through the rooftop access to elevators shafts, she sent them down the long way.

"Stairs?" she heard Alex muttering. "You've got to be kidding me."

"Sorry," Dr. Grey spoke into the intercom. "Can't take chances. Just...hold him tight and pretend he's your infirmed grandpa or something."

"Wonderful," Alex said. "Okay Granddad, down you go. You know, we could just shove him down the stairs or put a leash on him and drag him down behind us?"

"Whatever works, just don't kill him." Arcadia replied. "No cameras in there so I won't get the show either way. So just take your friend and go down three levels and on Sub-3, I'll buzz you through. Head down the hall, and there will be two more secured access doors you'll need clearance for, and then you'll find me."

She released the speaker button, then leaned back in her chair and returned her attention to the computer where she had various algorithms running to test Xander's solution. Matching protein strings vied against the prion strains in a simulated dance of give and take, the prions almost always overmatching anything thrown at them.

What is it, Xander, what am I missing? She chewed the end of a pencil, glaring down its length at the screen. *What were* you *missing?* Other than the obvious, that this was all theoretical on his part, smashed together on the fly while the island was exploding around him and he was locked in a room surrounded by zombies. He didn't have time to do real life tests or to fine-tune the equations. That was all up to her, and she was in the same situation, except here it was a whole city—hell, probably the whole country if not the world—crumbling around her.

No pressure.

She studied the interacting strands some more, then looked again at the other screen with Xander's formulae and conclusions. Shaking her head, she stood and headed to the other section of the room, to the lab where she called over two colleagues to help her prep the table with restraints.

"Let's move people, we've got a test subject coming down and this might be our only chance at this."

The others—a young woman named Marie, barely out of grad school, and an older man named Brian, with glasses and a grey pony tail who looked like he belonged out jamming with a folk band instead of in here with the world's most dangerous microbes, didn't move too fast to join her.

Their attention was still riveted on the main TV screen, set up in the corner of the lab beside wall-length freezer units and cabinets full of tools and slides and other equipment. Arcadia paused to watch the news feed—something she had resisted for most of the past hour, afraid of exactly the kind of reaction she was about to have.

Desperation, hopelessness, and complete disbelief.

"It can't be real," Marie said, echoing her thoughts.

As she waited for Alex and Veronica and the zombie specimen, Arcadia couldn't help but watch the live feed—shakier than a Blair Witch movie—as if it were found footage of a crowd of horrified civilians running down what looked to be Park Avenue in New York City. Towering buildings on all sides, yellow cabs parked or crashed and just left in place, blurry forms leaping onto others and tearing into them, shredding clothes and flesh; something in the distance: an unfocused shape, huge and hulking, barreling through the street and lowering great jaws to scoop up its prey, then howling into the smoke-filled sky. Other smaller bird-like creatures hurtled up and down, pulling the camera's focus mercifully up and away from the carnage on the streets.

For just a moment, Arcadia caught a glimpse of a helicopter up there around the rooftops, spinning helplessly, trying to shake off two of the bird-creatures. Then something huge loomed large in the camera's view, a scream pierced the audio, and the screen went black, turned to static and then... nothing for an uncomfortable few moments until another view took its place, this time of a sedate woman at a desk in a newsroom. Lights flickered overhead and her eyes darted around nervously.

"We have confirmation," she began, "that the White House is no more...destroyed and abandoned...that the president is dead and the alternate government, location undisclosed, has stepped in. We are assured that everything that can be done is being done, but can confirm at this time that the country is no longer being run from 1600 Pennsylvania Avenue. We are told...told again that the best course of action is to remain in your homes. Stay off the streets, lock your doors, hide in the basements if you can, and wait. Our troops are being mobilized...and we can only hope that this...infection hasn't spread to our bases in other more secure locations. We are told we can, and will, mount a counter offensive—we will quarantine those areas deemed already lost and..."

The woman shook her head. Her hands trembled and she obviously couldn't go on, but somehow mustered enough strength for one more thought before she got up and ran to the side, off camera.

"God save us."

#

Arcadia buzzed the trio into her secure lab, then re-secured the door and set the alarms. She briefly checked the screens and saw with alarm that a greater collection of zombies were congregating outside the main entrance and the side doors, probing, looking for ways in as if they smelled the last good meal left in the city.

Or were they here for some other reason?

She shook her head. That was being paranoid. These infected...they were mindless brutes, dead in most senses of the word except for the ability to move, and of course to feel hunger; but they were truly mindless, acting instinctively.

Or were they? They seemed to be drawn here to the CDC building, directed here for some reason.

"Were you followed?" she asked Alex as he led in the shambling, thrashing creature. She could sense its hunger, its raw animalistic nature, mixed with a primordial fearsomeness, and she trembled as if she stood before the ultimate predator.

"Followed?" Alex almost choked on the word. "I guess you could say that."

Veronica glanced over her shoulder as if expecting a mob of crazed zombies to be right behind them, clawing at the locked doors. "After we got our sports fan here, they seemed to all be on hyper-drive, coming at us from everywhere. Barely made it here without having to drop him and run." She let out a breath only after the specimen was deposited onto the table and strapped down with the help of the other two scientists. Veronica took a step back, wiped off her hands and then offered one to Arcadia.

"Special Agent Veronica Winters. Despite everything, I really am glad to meet you."

Arcadia reluctantly took the hand, thinking she'd have to immediately disinfect. "I imagine you know all about me."

The agent nodded. "Because of Xander Dyson. Yes. I had you monitored for a couple years in fact, in case he ever contacted you again."

"Slippery one, he was. Never gave a hint as to where the hell he was or what he was really up to. Even when we were together."

"Sorry," Veronica said with a shrug.

"No," Arcadia replied, softer. "I'm sorry. I know what he did. To your…"

"Let's not go there," Veronica interrupted. "We have a job to do, and every second here with them sniffing around the building is too long. They're going to get in soon—or else make it impossible for us to leave."

"How long do you need?" Alex asked.

Arcadia went to her workstation beside the thrashing, hissing creature on the table.

"We're about to find out." She looked up for a moment, back to Veronica. "Find out if Dyson actually sent me something that might atone for all the bad shit he did in his life."

"Can't believe he might be our last hope."

"Me either," Arcadia said, selecting a needle and preparing an injection. "But he was a damn genius, and given what's happening out there…." She looked up at the TV again, where new scenes of violence, smoking cities and mobilizing armed units flashed over and over.

"What's the latest?" asked Alex, taking his eyes off the captive now that it was finally secured. "Last we knew, major cities on the eastern coast were in trouble. It looks like Atlanta is done for… I'm sorry." He glanced at Marie, and then Brian, the one with the ponytail who looked even more ashen.

"We haven't heard from our families," he said.

Marie swallowed hard then spoke. "I had a friend text me that they were leaving with a National Guard convoy. Not sure where they're going. Into the Midwest."

"Safest bet," Alex agreed. He turned his attention to the screen, where the outline of the White House, in flames, stood like some surreal doomsday movie poster. "Washington?"

Arcadia shook her head.

"Gone. Transfer of power to the backup contingent, wherever they are."

"Hopefully NORAD in Colorado," Veronica said.

Alex turned and tapped the specimen on the forehead on its mask. "Where we have to take you, ASAP. Let's hurry this along."

"Wait," Marie said. "I think I heard there's finally going to be a press conference. Some kind of national announcement."

"About time," said Brian. "See if the new guy has a clue how to fix this."

"It's the Rapture," Marie said in a hollow voice. "No one can fix it."

"It's not the goddamned Rapture," Arcadia snapped, fixing the solution and prepping the needle, looking for a spot on the zombie's arm to insert it. "It's just an ancient mutated protein that's... raised the dead to devour the living and sent forth ancient devilish monsters..."

"The Rapture," Marie echoed, nodding her head. "Whatever you want to call it..."

"We're screwed," Brian voiced.

"Um, have some faith," Alex said. "We can beat this thing, or at least kill them all and sort it all out. First, though, someone has to accept that this was all planned. We were infected on purpose, a deliberate attack to wipe us out."

"Who would do that?" Marie asked, wide-eyed as she turned her attention to the screen again, where the American flag stood beside an empty podium. "Terrorists? ISIS?"

"No, try a greedy megalomaniac son of a..."

Alex's voice died and his heart skipped just as Veronica's hand found his in a flash and squeezed it like a vise.

"No way," they both said, staring at the TV, at the man in a pressed blue suit and power yellow tie who calmly walked up to the podium, smoothed back his silvery hair and turned a confident, smiling face upon the world.

"President?" Veronica said in a shaking voice that Arcadia imagined echoed a lifetime of disbelief and horror.

"DeKirk."

32.

Washington, D.C.

"Remington here. Are there any friendlies in the vicinity?"

Under cover of gloom and spreading dusk, weaving behind trees and abandoned cars, Remington occasionally tried his radio as he led his three soldiers across the back lawn, past the pool where the looming Washington Monument caught his attention for just a moment, a bleak sentinel now plastered with blood, basking in the last rays of the sun.

Remington didn't know whether to stop and stare, maybe salute, maybe cry. There was nothing else to do but run. They had escaped the bunker, finding an access tunnel that led in a serpentine route up and out through a non-descript guard post station, emerging through an unmarked door into its basement.

They put down two zombies upstairs, lurking about aimlessly, then saw their target across the way: another M1A1 tank, perhaps the one they had before, if it had been commandeered for additional duty.

"Looks to be still under our control," Remington noted, observing the dozen or so zombies crawling over it, screeching and trying to pry their way in. Another crylo bounded around the rear of the vehicle, staying away from its treads and its gun, but intent on waiting out the morsels inside.

"Let's lend a hand, men—and get us a ride out of here."

#

The technician took the handset and Remington surveyed the field one last time before dropping into the belly of the tank. He surveyed the littered corpses—including the dozen zombies he and his men had just put down, and the ragged mess of a carcass that used to be the crylo. Remington and another commando had emptied their clips into the thing's face and neck from point-blank, catching it as it raced at them over the side of the tank, screeching as if Remington could even hear over the M5's retort.

Now he dropped down and closed the hatch. Barked orders to his men and the other two that had held out in here as the tank crew.

"Let's get to work," he said as he sighted out the viewer.

"What are our orders?" one of the men asked.

Remington surveyed the Con, looking for where there would normally be a list of objectives and mission orders, parameters, but he only saw one: and just for all available F/A-18 fighter pilots…ordered to proceed to Atlanta and turn their missiles on a single set of GPS coordinates.

I bet I can guess where that is.

He swallowed hard, a lump in his throat. Maybe the only saving grace would be that most fighters had already been recalled to D.C. or New York and there wouldn't be any in Georgia available for the task. Or maybe he could get to the air first, and figure a way to countermand the order.

At first they were glad to change course because a horde of zombies blocked the way to the Capitol, complete with ptero escorts, but after about two miles of relatively easy progress toward the airport where they were able to gun down the opposition without stopping the tank, things became difficult.

Remington ordered his men to turn onto a highway. A multi-vehicle pileup of now abandoned cars and trucks obstructed all lanes, but being in a tank had its advantages and they were able to steamroll over and through barriers, only to be met with not one but a pair of storming *T. rex*es. The two tyrannosaurs ran at full speed down the concrete ribbon, pausing to snap at anything that moved. One plucked a man on a motorcycle desperately attempting to maneuver around wrecked cars from his seat and head-tossed him to the pavement where the other lizard stamped the human into a formless blood cake.

Remington directed his crew with steely resolve. "120 millimeter gun: Fire on left *T. rex*! 50-cal machine gun: Fire on right *T. rex*! Now! Fire, fire, fire! *Headshots*, people. Kill those things deader than shit, that's an order!"

But hitting the swinging heads of the zombie animals proved a difficult task. The tank's iconic big gun blasted a hole in the chest of one of the dinosaurs, ripping away one of the miniscule forearms, which landed on top of the tank and stayed there, still wriggling under some kind of localized neuronal network. Remington saw an opportunity.

He addressed the main gunner team. "Cut the legs out from under it. It'll still be alive but at least it won't be able to run." A succession of heavy rounds blasted into the animal's powerful hind legs, each one blowing part of the musculature away. Yet with each hit, the beast somehow took another giant step closer to the tank even as it fell lower, focusing the totality of its ire on the lone war machine.

Meanwhile, the machine guns peppered the other *T. rex* with hot fire, flaying the rotten skin from the creature's neck, chest and head. The first reptile finally succumbed to the heavy gunfire and flopped over onto the tank, clipping the other *T. rex* as it fell. That animal retaliated against its companion by snapping at its already wounded neck, opening it more, spilling its blood onto the dirt-caked armor.

The tank continued its momentum, rolled up and over the chest of the fallen *T. rex,* and then canted over sideways as it rolled off of the unpredictably contoured obstacle, landing on its side, the other tread in mid-air, churning uselessly.

Inside the tank, Remington fumed as he clutched at a ceiling handhold. "Call for any ground support or air support!" He scrambled out of the M1A1, nostrils twitching with the acrid tang of gunpowder and burnt flesh in the air.

He slid down from the tank and assessed his new surroundings, spotting a blue SUV not far away. He knew that many of these vehicles had simply been abandoned with keys inside once the sudden catastrophe began, so he ran up to the SUV, assessing its condition: tires were intact, windows too—at first glance it seemed functional.

When he looked inside the vehicle, though, Remington got quite the surprise. Two human zombies were tearing apart the driver of the vehicle, still belted in. He checked the rear but it was unoccupied. Just two human zombies gorging themselves on the open innards of a once good-looking middle-aged woman. Remington removed his service pistol. All of the windows were rolled up, but the passenger-side door was open. He didn't want to break a window on the vehicle, as he hoped to drive by shooting through it, so he pulled the driver door handle instead.

Locked. The pair of male zombies snapped their heads up to look at him but then resumed feasting, their bloodlust overcoming all else. Remington walked around to the open door. Took aim with his pistol. Put a neat circle in the forehead of one of the undead. The remaining zombie turned on him at that point, lunging, but Remington waited for the perfect shot to line up, then double-tapped it in the top of the skull.

He dragged all three of the corpses out of the vehicle and left them on the pavement nearby, a pile of wasted life. He moved to get inside the SUV but balked at the thought of sitting on so much blood and guts. He opened the back and checked to see if there were any towels or anything he could spread out on the seat. He found a small cache of roadside emergency equipment in the back, including a cheap yellow rain poncho. He ripped it from the bag and put it on, then got behind the wheel.

Would this thing start? The key was already in the ignition and he turned it, cracking a smile for the first time in a while as the consumer engine came to life. Then one of his men came running over to him, leaning in on the driver side as Remington put the window down.

"Major, what is your course of action, sir?"

"I have other orders. I'm taking this vehicle to the airport."

The soldier looked confused for a moment, glancing quickly back to the troubled tank before looking into the major's eyes. "Major, sir, what orders should I relay to the tank unit, sir? What about...us?"

Remington looked over at the carnage that enveloped his tank squad, draped in dead and dying resurrected prehistoric beasts, the wails of dying men carrying through the stench-filled air.

"Listen, soldier. I'm not going to lie. Things appear to be going from bad to worse real fast. As soon as you call for a medic team and backup, have the comm team work the radio bands—the short-waves, not the normal frequencies. Establish contact with groups of survivors, resistance factions, that kind of thing, some of whom might be distant. Don't assume help is coming soon. Call for it but don't get your hopes up. You may need to team up with bands of militia who are on our side. Get on those short-waves and enlist outside help."

His soldier registered the sheer gravity of his situation, then he gave a reluctant "Yes, sir!" He spun on a heel and ran back to the tank.

Remington maneuvered the SUV around the wreckage until he had a clear path down the highway. He allowed himself a weak smile as he scanned the road ahead. The airport loomed in the distance, relatively free from the chaos...and there were several planes, undamaged, resting in dying glow of the sun.

At least he had a ride waiting.

And he had orders to follow.

He had to get down there and save them. Save the original plan.

More than anything, more than his burning need to save his daughter and his wife, he had another mission, a larger imperative that only he could achieve.

He had to get to Atlanta and protect the cure.

33.

CDC, Atlanta

Veronica tried her best to tune out the droning voice of the man she had hunted for the better part of a decade. The man who had manipulated entire nations, who had duped the world and insinuated himself into a position he knew would thrust him into the role of President of the United States—and with it, she realized, grant him all the power he needed.

"He'll control the nukes," she said, not long after he began addressing the nation and the world, speaking in general terms about the great loss of life, the spread of the infection and the effectiveness of quarantines, and how everything that could be done was being done.

"And the armed forces," Alex said, letting the implications hang out there.

The other scientists noted their concern but didn't understand. "That's a good thing," Marie voiced. "Someone's in charge, someone's doing the right things, although why they haven't contacted us since the power transition, I don't know."

"They won't," Alex said, "because they don't care. *He* doesn't care."

"I don't understand," Arcadia said, after injecting the specimen, then standing back and checking the screens. The zombie had been hooked up to monitors and intravenous sensors, and now the waiting would begin.

"All you need to know," said Veronica, "is that man is the bastard who hired Dyson in the first place. The one who financed the Antarctica expeditions, who located the preserved dinosaurs and the ancient microbes—prions—or whatever they are. He's the one who organized all this, he was behind the shipments of the infected onto our soil. The invasion was all his idea."

"What?" Marie and Brian both turned, open-mouthed.

"Now he's stepped in and basically taken control of the only opposition he might have faced." Alex shook his head in disgust but also grudging admiration. "It's genius, and before anyone has time to second guess him or try to stop him, he'll control the satellites, the armies, the aircraft carriers, the nukes." Alex's eyes widened with the realization. "Hell, he could even…"

"Nuke our own cities," Veronica supplied. "In the name of quarantining or preserving the rest of the country from the spread of the infection."

"Except that wouldn't be their purpose."

"What about the rest of the world?" Brian asked, incredulous, staring at DeKirk in a new light, as if the president had just donned the imperial robes of the Emperor from *Star Wars*.

"I don't think they will matter much," Veronica said, "unless we can stop this thing here. DeKirk will have planes loaded with infection vectors ready to go."

"He'll hit London, Paris, Berlin, Rome…" Alex closed his eyes and took his hand away from Veronica's, making a fist. "Moscow, Tehran, Tokyo…it doesn't matter. They won't be able to defend against this."

"All right," Arcadia snapped. "Working as fast as I can. Would be nice if we had some other hope, but right now we are in doomsday—I'm sorry, Marie—Rapture mode. We train for this, we're ready for it. The Superbugs, the infectious diseases that might blindside us when we least expect it. Influenza and smallpox almost did us in a hundred years ago. Bubonic plague, Ebola, swine flu. This is nothing different."

"Except that we've lost control of it already," Marie said. "Look at the screens. Look out the window—if we had one."

"And," Brian said dully, "don't forget the fucking dinosaurs."

Arcadia stabbed the specimen with another needle, this time drawing out blood, which she brought quickly to a microscope. "Be quiet a moment, and focus here. Something Dyson missed. It looks like the protein sequences aren't responding to the introduction of the prions."

"Not responding?" Veronica asked. "I thought the prion things were the aggressors. That they took over, infected, blocked receptors, whatever."

"They're the Borg of the microbial world," Alex said with a loopy grin that no one except Brian shared, and Veronica desperately hoped they wouldn't high-five each other.

"Yes but in this case…no interest. They're not…" She looked up, eyes wide. "Bonding!"

"Huh?" Veronica asked, her attention drawn again to the TV where DeKirk had just finished saying something perfectly normal-sounding and confidence-building, like *May God bless our nation and our brave men and women as we endure through this crisis…*

"It needs a bonding agent!" Arcadia said, clapping her hands and then rushing to a cabinet. "Oh, please let it be that simple!"

"What's a bonding agent?" Alex asked.

"Something to cause that initial attraction between the protein strings. If they're not interested, this will bring them together."

"Ah," he said. "Kind of like alcohol at a singles bar."

Veronica rolled her eyes, but Arcadia actually let out a little laugh as she returned with a medicine dropper and a jar full of a clear liquid. "Exactly. It removes the inhibitions, and allows the attraction to commence."

She returned to the microscope and the blood spatter, again ignoring the zombie specimen—which seemed to be growing more agitated, kicking, thrashing and twisting its head back and forth. Snapping noises and grinding teeth from under the plastic mask did nothing to help Veronica's mood, but at least the CDC investigator seemed unfazed.

"There, now…" Arcadia peered into the microscope, and the next few moments, amidst the gnashing of teeth and the strains of the National Anthem playing on the TV as DeKirk made his exit, stage left, were tense as any Veronica could recall. She met Alex's eyes, and she was sure they shared the same thought: the next words out of Dr. Grey's mouth might spell the fate of human civilization.

Arcadia looked up, wide-eyed, but didn't give them the satisfaction.

"What is it?" Marie asked.

Without responding, Arcadia grabbed a new syringe, pulled out some of the Dyson solution, then sucked in a few drops of the bonding agent, and returned to the thrashing corpse—and promptly stuck the syringe into a vein in its neck.

She stood back after emptying the contents, and pressed her hands together.

Veronica stepped in closer along with Alex and their hands found each others' again, and this time they clenched out of need and trust and for the first time in a while...hope.

The zombie suddenly sucked in a huge wheezing breath. Its back arched at an impossibly strong angle until just its wrists and shins were straining against the table, and then just as quickly, all the energy seemed to flee, deflating from its lungs in a huge gasp—and then it sunk and lay completely still.

The vitals monitor—which had been registering brain waves as well as a flatline for heart rate and blood pressure, with values previously almost off the chart—now sunk in a sharp downward spike, then leveled out, flatlined along with the others.

Marie edged closer ahead of the rest, impatient. Her eyes were wide. "Is it—?"

"Dead? Cured?" Alex stepped in too, bringing Veronica with him.

She pulled back though. *I've seen this movie before. The thing which should be dead but isn't. And the expendable cast member...* She was about to warn Marie. Warn Brian, warn the research director. There was no way, they couldn't be this lucky, or this good. Dyson's cure—nothing so worthy of salvation could have come from that unholy monster.

No way, it was all some kind of unlucky trick, and they couldn't fall for it. Couldn't—

But then the impossible happened. Only it was much worse than she had feared.

One moment she registered the shock of hearing something overhead that sent shockwaves all the way down here, something that sounded like a muffled explosion on the order of a bunker-buster bomb.

In the next instant, the lights flickered, the glass doors shattered, the ceiling split open and a thousand tons of concrete, plaster and sand came collapsing down upon them.

34.

Nearly an hour after leaving Washington, D.C. airspace, Major Remington's F/A-18 streaked into the darkened, smoke-filled skies above Atlanta. Cutting his acceleration, he banked hard, then came in low over the suburbs and into the city, over the Superdome where he could barely make out fires and what looked like a packed stadium…only full of the dead and those feasting upon the soon-to-be-dead.

He tore ahead, then zeroed in on his objective. CDC Headquarters, target of all the other fighters scrambled from nearby locations. Another few seconds and he'd be within range, and hopefully there first, hopefully…

"Target destroyed," came the hollow voice on his comm. "Direct hit to the lower foundation with bunker-buster AT-201."

"No…" Remington rose above the plane coming toward him, the one having just finished the mission he had desperately intended to thwart, one way or another. He had imagined verbally trying to call rank on whoever was in the air, and barring that, would have reverted to shooting the other pilots out of the sky if he had to, anything to stop this mission and buy Agent Winters the time she needed to see that bio-solution through.

He banked around a taller building, came in low and saw for himself.

The target was collapsing, tumbling in on itself in a massive scene of destruction. Just…annihilated.

"Son of a bitch, *no…*" He flew low, into the rising smoke, then up and accelerating, turned and came back around, searching the area, checking the radar, trying to see through the debris and the smoke.

Was there any chance they survived? Could anybody survive that?

He clenched his jaw so tight he tasted blood. *Did they make it out first?*

The skies flashed red with an explosion somewhere a few miles to the east, where he had seen a contingent of tanks and armored vehicles, some sort of perimeter.

He turned and headed thoughtlessly in that direction, ignoring the next directive that came over his frequency: "All units return to Savannah AFB for refuel and next assignment."

"Copy, Savannah AFB," came three replies from the other birds in the air, and Remington saw their units on his radar, breaking off their trajectories and veering out together.

Let them go, he thought. *They don't know any better.* Following orders, he thought, and he shivered wondering what their next orders would be. Or would they land, only to be savaged by waiting hordes of undead? Would the faux-president continue to use the human forces at his disposal to knock out key resistance installations and soften the remaining population—all while keeping his brave colleagues in the dark?

Remington couldn't fathom the depths of the cruel, callous planning, the true scope of the evil that had triumphed today.

He could only do what he knew he had to do.

Disobey orders first and foremost, and second, provide aid to that contingent of humans making their last stand down there, against...

Remington squinted as he flew low over the buildings and avenues, over the apartments and parks and train station, the college campus and the libraries and the burning airport. He saw the mob of faster-than-life figures, dinosaurs loping in and among their ranks, all converging on the makeshift perimeter and the guards holding fast against the legions of Hell bearing down upon them as they protected several hundred civilians, huddled behind cars and barricades.

Remington got on his shortwave and tried to reach anyone down there in charge, promising what support he could give as he buzzed overhead, then prepared for another pass, right over their heads and into the oncoming army of undead.

He armed his missiles, readied the twin machine guns and came in low, sighting for the larger masses—and the goddamned dinosaur things.

He wouldn't let them advance without shredding their ranks a bit first and providing those warriors down there every chance at survival.

As he prepared to fire, something else caught his attention: something huge showing up on radar. A click ahead, previously lost in the darkness and behind other large buildings and blocks of skyscrapers.

Its enormous head rounded a corner, and Remington got a glimpse of a draconic visage: fiery crimson eyes, a long snout and slavering jaws, crustaceous horns and jagged carapace.

The other side had backup too.

New plan, Remington thought, firing automatic rounds and spitting terror down upon the undead, hopefully shattering enough skulls or at least incapacitating enough of them to give the National Guard an easier time of things.

Got to save the missiles for this other sonofabitch.

He angled up, plotted a new course and armed the heat-seekers, even as the dreadnought reared up and howled out a challenge, sensing its brothers in danger.

Come on, just another second 'til the Sidewinders are armed, and then you're history again—

A red blip streaked at a 90 degree angle on his radar and Remington had no time to even curse his stupidity—or rue the unfairness of being denied just one touch of good luck.

Another second was all he needed, but it wasn't to be.

A pterodactyl—something he had almost forgotten all about—soared across and intercepted his fighter like a rival, colliding with its beak and slamming hard and instantaneously ripping the wings and fuselage free. The missile launched but went straight down, impossible to correct, and exploded into the street, obliterating half a block of cars and stores.

Remington spun and spun, unable to scream, grunt or even cry out in agony. The auto-system kicked in and with the next 360, as he wildly cartwheeled and had no idea if he was on an upward trajectory or down, unable to read his gyro, the eject seat blasted out and shot him flying into the night, free from his plane and from the winged monstrosity howling at the escape of its prey.

Remington had a fleeting moment of serenity as he sailed over the tortured cityscape, looking back at his jet—bursting into an orange fireball and killing the ptero. He saw the hulking dreadnought thudding in the opposite direction, *slouching toward*

Bethlehem? The thought crashed through his mind giddily, just as he realized his chute wasn't opening, maybe because he had just crunched through the glass wall of a fifty-story bank building.

His helmet cushioned the impact somewhat, but then he barreled through the drop ceiling, which served to slow him down until connecting with a girder, twisting and dropping back onto the office floor and tumbling another thirty feet, knocking over office chairs and desks until coming to a stop in a darkened cubicle with a picture of smiling family members overlooking a pile of work folders, tomorrows to-do list which would never get done.

Remington tried to move, but couldn't feel a thing, couldn't think, couldn't breathe.

Everything turned black, the curtain closing on his life, and his daughter's face appeared for a brief moment as she pulled away from him, eyes downcast and a tear slipping free.

The world was burning, and the dead held sway across all.

As he descended into the darkness, he held onto one thought, desperately clinging to it for all he was worth…that the cure, if there was one…was buried here in this city along with him.

Because like all buried things lately, nothing stayed down for long.

END

To be continued in JURASSIC DEAD 3

CHECK OUT OTHER GREAT ZOMBIE NOVELS

Z BURBIA
by Jake Bible

Whispering Pines is a classic, quiet, private American subdivision on the edge of Asheville, NC, set in the pristine Blue Ridge Mountains. Which is good since the zombie apocalypse has come to Western North Carolina and really put suburban living to the test!

Surrounded by a sea of the undead, the residents of Whispering Pines have adapted their bucolic life of block parties to scavenging parties, common area groundskeeping to immediate area warfare, neighborhood beautification to neighborhood fortification.

But, even in the best of times, suburban living has its ups and downs what with nosy neighbors, a strict Home Owners' Association, and a property management company that believes the words "strict interpretation" are holy words when applied to the HOA covenants. Now with the zombie apocalypse upon them even those innocuous, daily irritations quickly become dramatic struggles for personal identity, family security, and straight up survival.

ZOMBIE RULES
by David Achord

Zach Gunderson's life sucked and then the zombie apocalypse began.

Rick, an aging Vietnam veteran, alcoholic, and prepper, convinces Zach that the apocalypse is on the horizon. The two of them take refuge at a remote farm. As the zombie plague rages, they face a terrifying fight for survival.

They soon learn however that the walking dead are not the only monsters.

CHECK OUT OTHER GREAT ZOMBIE NOVELS

900 MILES
by S.Johnathan Davis

John is a killer, but that wasn't his day job before the Apocalypse.

In a harrowing 900 mile race against time to get to his wife just as the dead begin to rise, John, a business man trapped in New York, soon learns that the zombies are the least of his worries, as he sees first-hand the horror of what man is capable of with no rules, no consequences and death at every turn.

Teaming up with an ex-army pilot named Kyle, they escape New York only to stumble across a man who says that he has the key to a rumored underground stronghold called Avalon..... Will they find safety? Will they make it to Johns wife before it's too late?

Get ready to follow John and Kyle in this fast paced thriller that mixes zombie horror with gladiator style arena action!

WHITE FLAG OF THE DEAD
by Joseph Talluto

Millions died when the Enillo Virus swept the earth. Millions more were lost when the victims of the plague refused to stay dead, instead rising to slaughter and feed on those left alive. For survivors like John Talon and his son Jake, they are faced with a choice: Do they submit to the dead, raising the white flag of surrender? Or do they find the will to fight, to try and hang on to the last shreds or humanity?

CHECK OUT OTHER GREAT ZOMBIE NOVELS

VACCINATION
by Phillip Tomasso

What if the H7N9 vaccination wasn't just a preventative measure against swine flu?

It seemed like the flu came out of nowhere and yet, in no time at all the government manufactured a vaccination. Were lab workers diligent, or could the virus itself have been man-made? Chase McKinney works as a dispatcher at 9-1-1. Taking emergency calls, it becomes immediately obvious that the entire city is infected with the walking dead. His first goal is to reach and save his two children.

Could the walls built by the U.S.A. to keep out illegal aliens, and the fact the Mexican government could not afford to vaccinate their citizens against the flu, make the southern border the only plausible destination for safety?

ZOMBIE, INC
by Chris Dougherty

"WELCOME! To Zombie, Inc. The United Five State Republic's leading manufacturer of zombie defense systems! In business since 2027, Zombie, Inc. puts YOU first. YOUR safety is our MAIN GOAL! Our many home defense options - from Ze Fence® to Ze Popper® to Ze Shed® - fit every need and every budget. Use Scan Code "TELL ME MORE!" for your FREE, in-home*, no obligation consultation! *Schedule your appointment with the confidence that you will NEVER HAVE TO LEAVE YOUR HOME! It isn't safe out there and we know it better than most! Our sales staff is FULLY TRAINED to handle any and all adversarial encounters with the living and the undead". Twenty-five years after the deadly plague, the United Five State Republic's most successful company, Zombie, Inc., is in trouble. Will a simple case of dwindling supply and lessening demand be the end of them or will Zombie, Inc. find a way, however unpalatable, to survive?

22522957R00126

Made in the USA
Middletown, DE
04 August 2015